A Long Way From Home

A Long Way From Home

Alice Walsh

Second Story Press

Library and Archives Canada Cataloguing in Publication

Walsh, Alice (E. Alice)
A long way from home / by Alice Walsh.

Issued also in an electronic format.
ISBN 978-1-926920-79-5

1. September 11 Terrorist Attacks, 2001—
Juvenile fiction. I. Title.

PS8595.A5847L66 2012   jC813'.54   C2012-904022-3

Edited by Kathryn Cole
Copyedited by Lynda Guthrie
Designed by Melissa Kaita

Cover photos © iStockphoto

Printed and bound in Canada

*Second Story Press gratefully acknowledges the support of the Ontario Arts Council
and the Canada Council for the Arts for our publishing program. We acknowledge
the financial support of the Government of Canada through the Canada Book Fund.*

ONTARIO ARTS COUNCIL
CONSEIL DES ARTS DE L'ONTARIO

Canada Council Conseil des Arts
for the Arts du Canada

Published by
SECOND STORY PRESS
20 Maud Street, Suite 401
Toronto, ON M5V 2M5
www.secondstorypress.ca

In Memory of
Steven Wallace Maynard (1980–2003)
and William Joseph. (B.J.) Maynard (1983–1988)

Gander, Newfoundland
September 11, 2001

Rabia stared out the plane window, her stomach knotted in fear. They had been parked on the runway for hours, a long way from New York where the plane was supposed to land after leaving from London. She glanced at her nine-year-old brother, Karim, who sat perfectly still, his hands folded in his lap.

Mama was on the other side of Karim, her face creased into a worried frown. "What is wrong?" she whispered anxiously. "Why have they taken us to this place?"

"I don't know," Rabia replied. But something *was* wrong. She could tell by the anxious faces of the passengers pacing the narrow aisle. Others sat perfectly still in their seats, fear etched on their faces. Through the window, Rabia could see people lining the fence around the airport. Once in a while, she caught a glimpse of men in dark uniforms with yellow stripes on the legs and arms. Their hats had a band of yellow as well. They were circling the plane with big dogs.

Rabia had picked up bits of information from the other passengers. *Hijack* was a word one man used. Father had once told her about people being taken hostage on airplanes. Sometimes the hostage takers threatened to kill the passengers if they didn't get what they wanted. Rabia shuddered and reached for Karim's hand.

She glanced across the aisle at the American boy who had boarded the plane with his mother when it stopped to refuel and pick up more passengers in London. His longish blond hair was cut like the actor in the movie *Titanic*. Colin, his mother had called him. For most of the trip he had either played with some kind of gadget or read a book. Now he was staring out the window, frowning. His mother had her face hidden in her hands as if she was in terrible pain.

"What do you suppose is happening?" Rabia heard the boy ask his mother.

She rubbed her temples, her face pale. "I don't know, Colin," she said. Colin slumped down in his seat, and picked up the book he had been reading.

"Can I get you something?" A steward stood in the aisle, smiling at Rabia. With his dark skin and even white teeth, he reminded her of Amir.

A Long Way From Home

Dear Amir, Rabia thought, fighting back tears as she recalled the last day she'd spent with her older brother.

Chapter 1
Kabul, Afghanistan—August 2000

"I'm going to the market for ice cream," Amir called. "Would anyone like to come with me?"

Rabia was sitting on the floor with Karim, trying to interest him in building a bridge with stones and blocks of wood. "Would you like to go with Amir?" she asked.

Karim looked at her, a blank stare on his face.

Rabia felt a stab of sadness. There was a time when her brother would have jumped at the chance to go for ice cream. But now Karim had lost interest in everything. Less than a year ago, he had watched as their oldest brother, Yousef, was killed. Since that day, he had not uttered a word. *Poor little brother,* Rabia thought. She could only imagine what he'd witnessed, and it tore at her heart.

Rabia took his hand and helped him to his feet. "I'm sure Karim would like to go with you, Amir."

"Are you coming too, little sister?"

Rabia shook her head, although she wanted more than anything to get out of the house. "It's too hot," she said. "I would suffocate under the *burqa* in this heat." Besides, it was nearly impossible to eat ice cream inside a burqa. And she would have to stand outside the store or eat in a separate area apart from her brothers.

Amir squeezed her shoulder. "I will bring you back a treat," he promised.

"Thanks, Amir."

"How about you, Mama?" Amir asked, turning his attention to their mother, who was sitting quietly on a mattress.

Mama shook her head. "Go and have fun, children." She gave them a weak smile.

Rabia watched her brothers leave, feeling a twinge of envy. Boys had so much more freedom than girls. They could wander all over Kabul with heads, arms, and legs bare. Rabia spent days on end stranded at home with nothing to do. It had been six months since she'd started wearing the burqa. She hated it. Peering through the mesh of tiny holes across the front was like looking through the bars of a prison. The cap felt like a band of rubber squeezing her head, giving her dreadful headaches. The outfit covered her whole body, including her hands and feet. It was difficult to walk, and women often stumbled and fell. It was especially difficult for Rabia who had lost her foot to a landmine and had been fitted with a prosthesis. The artificial foot was poorly made in the first place, but now she had grown and it chaffed badly, making her leg sore. Still, she supposed she was lucky to have it. Many others who had suffered the same fate in Afghanistan had to manage with nothing.

Rabia pursed her lips. Why did the Taliban have so much hatred for girls and women? Why were they making their lives so difficult?

Crossing the room, she knelt to remove a loose floorboard. Beneath it were boxes filled with books, photographs, magazines, and CDs — things forbidden by the Taliban. Her family could be severely punished for possessing such things.

Rabia reached into one of the boxes and pulled out a delicate gold bracelet. It was a gift from Father on the day she was born, and it was her most cherished treasure. *To my Rabia on her birthday* was engraved on the inside. She fought back tears. It had been many months since Father was arrested, and his absence was an aching wound inside her. In many Afghan families the father doted on the sons. But there was no doubt that Rabia's father was proud of her.

Mama favored her sons, something Rabia knew but found hard to understand. She could do all the things her brothers did. Even with her artificial foot, she could play soccer and run fast. And she learned things much quicker than her brothers. Father often said she was like a sponge, soaking up information.

Father had taught her English and boasted about how easily she picked up the language. He knew there was no future for his children in Afghanistan. He wanted to prepare them should they have a chance to leave their country some day. Her brothers spoke the language haltingly, but to Rabia it came as naturally as breathing.

She dug into one of the boxes and found a large envelope crammed with photographs. Not so long ago, Mama had been the best portrait photographer in all of Kabul. She ran a studio that she was quite proud of. People came from all over the country to have their pictures taken.

Inside the envelope, Rabia found portraits of herself and her brothers when they were babies and pictures of Father when he was younger. There was a photo of Mama wearing a short skirt, her long hair hanging loose. In another, she was standing on the street wearing jeans and a short jacket. Rabia glanced quickly from the image of the young girl to the weary, broken-down woman seated before her. There were now lines in her face, and her hair was streaked with gray. Since Father's arrest and Yousef's death, Mama seemed to have no life left in her.

Rabia felt a rush of tenderness. Smiling, she held up the photograph. "Mama, you look beautiful," she said. "And you are not wearing a veil or headdress."

"Women won the right not to wear the veil back in 1964 — five years after the prime minister appeared in public with his wife and daughters unveiled." Mama smiled ruefully. "Of course the religious leaders never accepted it. They protested just as they did years later when education for girls became legal."

"Everything is so different now," Rabia said in an attempt to keep their conversation going.

"Yes, daughter, things have changed," Mama said and fell silent.

"Remember this one, Mama?" Rabia held up a picture of a sky filled with red, blue, orange, and green kites. "They look like bright colorful birds."

A look of sorrow crossed Mama's face, but she remained silent.

Disappointed, Rabia put the photographs back in the envelope.

She never tired of hearing Mama's stories about days gone by. She had fond memories of visits to the Kabul museum that displayed art from ancient cities around the world. Mama remembered a time before the

Soviet invasion, before civil war, before the Taliban and Al-Qaeda. That was before bombs destroyed the streets of Kabul. Before Yousef was killed. Before Father… Rabia's eyes brimmed. *What have they done with you, Father?* She cried silently. *Are you wasting away in some Taliban prison? Do you even know that Yousef was killed by a rocket? We had to bury him without his arms.*

Rabia swiped at her eyes with the heel of her palm. She missed the days when her family was together. The Sunday afternoons they drove to the countryside to visit relatives. Sometimes, they took trips to the Bamiyan Valley where the largest Buddha statues in the world were carved in the cliffs.

Those days are gone forever, Rabia thought sadly. The Taliban had ruined everything. She was barely seven years old when they seized Kabul. Big bearded bullies in black turbans, their wild eyes darkened with kohl. She had just started her second year at school and was learning to write and add numbers. Her teacher read them books and encouraged them to make up stories. She loved that magical time in her life.

Under Taliban rule, schools for girls were closed. Rabia and Karim were warned not make noise, not even to laugh. They were forbidden to sing the songs they had learned in school. Dancing, music, soccer, even flying kites was forbidden. They had to hide all their books and get rid of their television set. Father was forced to grow a beard. The burqa became mandatory, and women began drifting through the streets like blue clones. They could not go out in public unless escorted by a *mabram*, a male relative.

At first, Mama tried to make light of it. "How do you like my new outfit?" she would ask Rabia and her brothers. But more than once Rabia heard her complaining to Father. "How can I go anywhere shrouded in this body bag?"

As months went by, Mama became depressed. Rabia hated seeing her so sad. After a while, she refused to go out at all. She had terrible headaches and her legs and feet ached from arthritis. It was difficult for Rabia to see her proud, strong mother reduced to a shell of a woman, afraid of her own shadow.

Clenching her fists, Rabia felt a surge of resentment toward the Taliban. They burned paintings, books, photographs, and film. Mama was forced to close down her studio — the studio she loved and worked so hard for. "Ignorant, uncultured, thugs," she called them. "Art, music, and literature have always been a part of our rich heritage." But the Taliban went right on destroying. They even blew the arms and legs off the Buddha statues that had stood in the Bamiyan Valley for hundreds of years.

The door burst open, rousing Rabia from her musings. Amir rushed into the house followed by Karim. She had only to look at Amir's face to know something was wrong.

Mama rose quickly from the mattress. "Amir?" she said, her voice filled with concern. "What is it? Tell me, son, what is wrong?"

Chapter 2

"Did anyone follow you?"

Omar, their neighbor, sat across from Amir, a frown on his broad face. Mama had called on him after Amir and Karim returned from the market. Breathlessly, Amir told them what had happened. They were crossing the street when two Talibs approached, demanding to know why Amir had not joined the militia. Luckily, a ruckus on the other side of the street diverted their attention, and the boys were able to get away.

"Did anyone follow you?" Omar repeated, peering at Amir with concern.

Amir shook his head. "I don't know," he said. "I grabbed Karim's hand and ran."

Omar's frown deepened. Turning to Mama, he said, "Amir may be in immediate danger. He must leave tonight. I will help arrange it."

"Tonight?" Mama's face filled with anguish. "Must I lose Amir too?" she cried. "Is it not enough that Yousef was killed? That my husband was taken from me?" She glanced at Karim. "Is it not enough that my youngest child is so traumatized he can no longer speak? I have lost all my children."

I am still here, Mama, Rabia wanted to remind her. *I am only a daughter, but I am still your child.*

Amir kissed his mother's cheek. "Mama, we both knew this day would come," he said gently.

Rabia nodded. It had not been entirely unexpected. Amir was fourteen. For months now, the Taliban had been sweeping through the streets, drafting boys as young as eleven and twelve.

"I have to escape now, Mama," Amir said. "Surely you do not want me to join the Taliban militia."

"Never!" Mama shook her head fiercely. "Those brutes killed your brother. Arrested your father. I would rather die than see my a son of mine fight for them."

Rabia's eyes brimmed. She was going to miss her big brother. Amir was smart and funny; he cheered her up whenever she was feeling down. Another unsettling thought struck her. *What will we do without Amir's salary?* He worked as an apprentice for Latif the tailor. The small wage he earned went to pay rent and buy food and necessities for the family. It was the only income they had. The Taliban forbade women to work, so Rabia and Mama could never find jobs.

Omar stood up, his gaze on Mama. "I have relatives in Iran, Ayeesha," he said. "I will arrange for Amir to stay with them until he is settled." Turning to Amir, he said: "Pack a change of clothes and some food. I will return after dark."

Mama let out a long mournful sob.

"Amir is a good son." Omar laid a steadying hand on Mama's arm. "You are blessed," he said as he headed for the door.

Rabia heard the sadness in Omar's voice and knew he was thinking of his own son, Mahmood, who had greatly disappointed him. After his wife had died, Omar sent Mahmood to a *madrassa,* a religious school in Pakistan. He learned the Koran by heart, studied Shari'a and Islamic law, and was taught the beliefs of the prophet Mohammed. But Omar often complained that his only son had turned into a stranger overnight. He showed disrespect for his father and refused to obey him. It was out of the madrassa that the Taliban emerged. The last time Rabia saw Mahmood, she almost did not recognize him. He was patrolling the streets, a whip in his hand. With his turban and bushy beard, he looked bigger and meaner. For once, Rabia was glad she was hidden under the burqa.

Somewhere in the distance, a rocket crashed, jolting Rabia out of her thoughts.

Mama jumped nervously. "When is it going to end?" she cried. "Bombs and rockets have been falling for more than twenty years now."

Amir put a comforting arm around his mother's shoulder. "Shhh, Mama. It is going to be okay."

"Will they not stop until every man, woman, and child in Afghanistan is killed?" Mama continued.

Poor Mama, Rabia thought. *After all these years, she still isn't used to the bombs and rockets.*

Amir picked up a knapsack and began filling it with his clothes and belongings. Mama boiled eggs and rice for him to take on the journey. She took naan and cheese from the cupboard and filled a flask with water. All the while she cried openly, wiping her eyes on her sleeve.

• • •

Amir left the house a few minutes before midnight. Karim had fallen asleep, but Rabia stayed awake to see him off. By now, Mama's eyes were red and swollen. However, she accepted Amir's leaving with a quiet calm. "May Allah be with you, my son, and keep you safe," she said.

Rabia felt the sting of tears behind her eyelids, and bit down hard on her lip.

Amir held her close. "Take care of Mama, little sister," he whispered. "She will be depending on you."

Rabia hugged him fiercely.

"Latif the tailor still owes me wages," he told her. "They will help for a while." A shadow crossed his face. "Rabia, I think it would be best if you got out of Afghanistan. Try to convince Mama to leave." He frowned. "I should have taken care of it myself months ago."

Rabia squeezed his hand. She knew that as the oldest surviving son, Amir felt responsible for the family. "Don't worry, Amir. I will take care of things," she told her brother as he stepped out into the dark night.

Chapter 3
Spring 2001

Weeks went by. Summer gave way to fall. Before long, snow covered the streets and rooftops of Kabul. By the time spring rains washed away the snow, Mama had sold most of her jewelry. Although they were careful with their money, Rabia knew it would not last forever. She stayed awake at night worrying about what would happen when they had nothing left to sell. If they couldn't pay the rent, the landlord would turn them out.

Women and girls could not survive on the streets of Kabul. Amir was right; they had to leave. Rabia was terrified at the thought of the refugee camps in Pakistan — nothing more than tents in the open air, so close together they touched. She had heard stories of how people died from starvation or perished from the cold in such places. But what choice did they have? She was a girl, not yet fourteen, with a sick mother and a brother who could not speak.

After Father was arrested, Mama often cried in secret. After Yousef died, she made no attempt to hide her tears. But now she sat for hours, her face a frozen mask. At times, she didn't seem to realize Rabia and Karim were in the same room. Rabia brought her cups of tea and urged her to eat. She made sure Karim was fed and cared for.

Would Mama mind so much if I had left? Rabia wondered. She knew Mama loved her, but not the way she loved her sons. Rabia recalled her first week at school. "Your daughter is the brightest, most inquisitive child in the class," the teacher told Mama when she came to pick her up. Rabia felt so proud, her heart swelled. But Mama had merely shrugged. "It is my sons who will take care of me," she said. Rabia still couldn't think of that day without feeling a stab of rejection.

Rabia spent hours trying to get her little brother engaged in building things. Before Yousef was killed, Karim used to build bridges with books, stones, shoes — whatever he could find. "That boy is going to be a fine engineer some day," Father used to brag. But now Karim showed little interest in anything. *Both Mama and Karim are lost to me,* Rabia thought sadly.

It was late May when a letter arrived from Mama's sister. For years there had been no real mail service in

Kabul, and this was hand-delivered by some traveler. "A letter from Aunt Roxanne!" Rabia cried excitedly, as she tore open the envelope. Her aunt lived in Quetta, a city near the Pakistan border. After Uncle was killed, Aunt Roxanne moved there with her daughter, Sima. There had been no contact with her since.

The letter said that a relief organization was coming to Pakistan. They were sending refugee widows and their children to live in the United States. Roxanne urged her sister to come to Pakistan and apply for the program.

Rabia clasped the letter to her chest. It was the answer to her prayers. "Mama," she said. "This is our chance to escape."

"We are not refugees, child."

"But Mama, don't you see? If we go to Pakistan, we *will* be refugees," Rabia reasoned. "We will have to leave Afghanistan sooner or later. Now is the time."

"My child, what will we do in America?" Mama asked wearily. "I am *not* a widow. Your father will come back someday looking for us."

It was true. Mama was not officially a widow. Like a lot of women whose husbands had been arrested, she had no idea if Father was dead or alive. But as much as Rabia hoped and prayed for his return, she knew they could not wait for him. She couldn't let an opportunity like this pass. "Mama," she said patiently, "We *have* to do this. We cannot stay in Afghanistan any longer. It is too dangerous."

"What about Amir?"

Rabia peered into her mother's anxious face. "We will let everyone know where we're going," she said. "When Amir and Father return, the neighbors will tell them where we are."

Mama looked doubtful.

Rabia gestured toward the tiny window, the only one in the house that did not have boards nailed across its frame. Women in burqas moved through the narrow, dusty street like ghosts. Dirty, barefoot children in tattered clothing trailed after them, their arms as thin as sticks. They were widows and orphans begging for food and money. The women were not allowed to work, yet they would be severely punished if the Taliban caught them begging. "Look. That could be us months from now," Rabia told Mama.

Rabia had seen how the Taliban punished women. Shortly after they had seized Kabul, she was out walking with Father when they chanced upon two Talibs beating a woman. Rabia couldn't imagine what crime the poor woman had committed to be beaten so savagely. Father had whisked his daughter away. She remembered sobbing against his chest while he carried her through the streets. Even now, she trembled at the memory.

But Mama came up with one excuse after another not to leave. For weeks, Rabia pleaded, argued, tried to reason. "Father would want it," she told her mother time and time again. Finally, Mama relented.

• • •

Mama sold the last of her jewelry to pay the bus and train fare. Omar agreed to exchange the money for roupees, and offered to escort them to the bus station.

Rabia lifted the floorboard, and dug out their boxes of possessions. They could take very little with them, and books, magazines, and CDs would have to be left behind. Carefully, she took out the bracelet her father had given her. It would be easy to hide. But what about all the beautiful pictures Mama had taken over the years? Rabia could not bear to leave them behind. All she had left to remember Yousef, Amir, and Father were photographs. She found a cotton drawstring pouch and placed the envelope of photographs in it. She would carry the bag inside her burqa, she decided. The Taliban never looked under a woman's burqa.

Rabia looked sadly at Father's cherished books. Her father loved books, and at one time had shelves filled with them. He read them stories from Rudyard Kipling and poems by Afghan poets.

Father used to teach poetry at the University of Kabul. After the university closed down, he held a poetry workshop in their home. Every Tuesday afternoon women came with books and notepads hidden inside their burqas. At first Mama was against it. "If the Taliban find out, they will put us in prison," she protested.

"I have to give the women hope," Father said. "Without hope they will fall into despair. Besides," he added, "we cannot let those thugs take away *all* our freedom."

In time, Mama came to enjoy the workshops as much as the students did. Rabia too, listened with interest as they discussed various poets and their work. She especially liked the poetry of Rabia Balkhi, the first female Persian poet, and Rabia's namesake. A princess who lived in the ninth century, Rabia Balkhi fell in love with a slave named Baktash and wrote beautiful poetry for him. When her brother found out about her love for the slave, he cut her jugular vein and left her to die. As her life ebbed away, she wrote her last love poem for Baktash in her own blood. Father often said Rabia symbolized the perseverance of the Afghan women.

It is an honor to have the name of such a brave woman, Rabia thought as she lifted the lid of another box from under the floor. On top, was the old doll she had carried everywhere before the Taliban came. In the same box, she found a video encased in plastic. It was the film *Titanic* that had been smuggled across the border from Iran. At one time, the movie was celebrated in Kabul, and her parents used to organize "Titanic parties." Groups of friends would go to a house that had a forbidden television and watch the movie. Rabia often heard her mother discussing the film with friends. It was about the huge ocean liner that sank when it ran into an iceberg. But it was the love story between the characters Jack and Rose that held everyone's attention.

Titanic became so popular in Kabul that in the marketplace, merchants named clothes, furniture, even fruit and vegetables after the ship. Stallholders would call out, "Get your Titanic melons here." Bakers would shout, "We have Titanic baklava baked fresh this morning." Boys who had seen the movie would go into barber shops and ask for a "Titanic hair cut," so they could look like Leonardo DiCaprio, the actor who played Jack.

Smiling, Rabia shook her head. She was about to put the film back in the box, but on impulse, slipped it into her pouch.

Chapter 4
June 2001

"This is it," the driver said, pulling the bus over to the side of the road. "The Pakistan border is just up ahead."

"How far?" someone asked.

"About half a mile down this road."

Clutching their bundles, Rabia and her family followed the other passengers off the bus. Rabia looked at the long stretch of road ahead of her. Exhausted by the heat and the long bus ride, she wanted only to find a place to sit. Her leg ached, and her head was starting to throb. She took her brother's hand. "Are you tired, Karim?"

He did not respond.

"How are you, Mama?" Rabia asked, turning to her mother. Mama looked too weary to take another step.

"It has been a long trip, daughter." Her face was

furrowed in pain, and Rabia knew her arthritis was bothering her.

"We are almost there, Mama."

By now, they had slipped off their burqas and covered their hair and shoulders with *chadors*. This was still risky because the Taliban controlled the area around the Pakistan border. But the long scarves were so light compared to the burqas that Rabia couldn't help feeling better.

As they walked farther down the road, the crowd thickened. There were young people and old people, mothers with babies on their back. Like Rabia, many people had arms, legs, hands, or feet missing. Everyone looked exhausted.

"We are almost there," Rabia whispered, as much to encourage herself as the others. The two-day bus ride over steep mountains and through rocky gorges had been brutal. At times, she expected the bus to go off a cliff and land in the valley below. She trembled whenever they came to a Taliban checkpoint and couldn't bear to think of what would happen if her pouch with the forbidden film and photographs was discovered. Hoisting her bundle, she tried not to think of that as they made their way down the dusty desert road toward the border.

Eventually, they came to a gate flanked by two buildings. Rabia's mouth dropped open. Hundreds of people were clamoring to get inside. She had not expected it to be so crowded.

Uniformed guards stood at the gate. "Stand back!" one of them ordered. He was a big man who swung a baton whenever the crowd surged toward the gate.

Rabia watched, feeling a wave of hopelessness. What chance did they stand of getting past the guards? How were they to enter Pakistan if they could not even approach the gate? The country had closed its borders in 1978 after millions of Afghans fled to escape the Soviets. Still, people went there all the time, didn't they? Aunt Roxanne must have thought it was still possible.

What do we do now? Rabia wondered. Already the sun was starting to go down, filling the desert with shadows. Around her, people had spread mats, shawls, and blankets on the ground. Rabia found a place next to a family who had two children, a boy and a girl. The girl looked to be a little younger than Rabia; the boy was about Karim's age. "We will have to spend the night here," she told Mama.

Mama merely nodded.

They ate the last of their naan and cheese. Mama laid her head on the ground and after a few minutes fell asleep. Karim had gone off to some unreachable place inside himself. Around her, Rabia heard a babble of conversations in various Afghan languages: Pashtu, Dari,

Uzbec. *Tomorrow I will have to come up with a plan,* she told herself. *There must be some way to get inside Pakistan.*

The family sitting next to them seemed friendly, and after some time they struck up a conversation. The mother and father, Zoya and Sayeed, were Hazara people who had traveled from the province of Bamiyan. The Taliban bore a particular hatred for the Hazares, and often killed them for no good reason. Rabia could understand why Sayeed was anxious to get his family out of Afghanistan.

"I didn't expect it to be this crowded," Rabia admitted. "I don't know how we are going to get inside."

"Tonight we are headed for the mountains," Zoya said. "We will enter Pakistan from there."

"The mountains?"

Zoya nodded. "It will take about three days and it is very dangerous."

There were wild animals in the mountains, but most likely Zoya was thinking of the thieves and bandits who roamed the area. Rabia looked down at her artificial foot. It would be difficult, but she could make it if she had to. She never let her "handicap" get in the way of anything she wanted to do. But then she glanced at Mama, who was asleep beside her. *No,* she decided. *It is out of the question. Mama would never make it through the mountains. Not with her arthritis and swollen feet.*

"There may be another way," said Sayeed, who had been quietly listening to their conversation.

Rabia looked up at him hopefully.

"But you will need money," he continued.

"Money?" Rabia felt the glimmer of hope leak away. What little money they had left would be needed for the train to Quetta, for cab fare, and food.

Sayeed tilted his head toward the gate. Rabia followed his gaze. She noticed a smaller opening, off to one side of the main gate, where people were quietly approaching the guard. It took her a moment to understand he was accepting bribes. Rabia's heart quickened. *How much money would we need?*

"It is not cheap," Sayeed said, as if reading her thoughts. "A friend of mine paid two thousand roupees."

Rabia shook her head, all hope gone. That was more money than they had. *There has to be another way,* she told herself.

That night, while everyone else was sleeping, Rabia tossed and turned. Had they come this far for nothing? They could not stay at the border forever. What would they do if they couldn't get into Pakistan? Returning to Kabul was out of the question.

Rabia was still awake when Zoya and her family got up for their long trek over the mountains. It was past midnight, and the moon and stars were shrouded with thick clouds. Rabia listened as they moved quietly in the darkness, gathering their belongings.

"May Allah bless you, sister," Sayeed said before they left.

"Have a safe journey," Rabia told them. "I will pray to Allah to keep you safe." Rabia watched with envy as Sayeed put his arm around his daughter's shoulder.

She thought of her own father, her throat tightening with longing. A wave of loneliness swept through her. She needed Father's gentle wisdom to guide her in this difficult time. Not so long ago, she had been a child depending on her parents. Now she felt as if the weight of the world had settled on her shoulders.

All night long, Rabia lay on the hard ground picturing Father's face, imagining the words he might say to her. By the time she drifted into a troubled sleep, she had a plan that might work. *It is our only chance*, she told herself.

• • •

When Rabia awoke, it took her a few moments to realize where she was. Mama was still sleeping. Karim sat nearby, staring vacantly at the people around him.

"Mama, wake up." Rabia shook her mother. "I have a plan."

Less than ten minutes later, they were standing at the gate. A fat man in a uniform frowned at them. He had a thick neck and small eyes like raisins.

Rabia swallowed back her fear. "My family…we would like to go to Pakistan."

"Where are your passports?" the guard demanded.

Rabia's mouth went dry, but she forced out the words. "We do not have passports."

The guard eyed her suspiciously.

With trembling hands, Rabia opened her pouch, and took out her treasured bracelet. "But I do have this."

The guard took the bracelet. "Are you offering it to me?" He seemed amused.

Rabia's pulse was pounding, her palms sweating. "It is gold and very valuable. It should fetch a good price in the marketplace."

The guard examined the bracelet closely. Rabia wanted to snatch it from his pudgy fingers. It was her bracelet, her gift from Father. It had her name engraved on it. But she knew Father would say that this was no time to be sentimental.

"We are all alone, and except for my little brother, we do not have males in the family."

The border guard smiled, a glint in his eye.

Rabia held her breath.

"Okay, little sister," he said. "I am a kind man with a

kind heart. Since you have no males to protect you, I will let you through."

"Thank you," Rabia whispered as she gestured for Mama and Karim to follow her. Already, the guard was pocketing her treasured bracelet.

Without another glance back, Rabia walked though the gate that would lead to freedom.

Chapter 5

"Is this it?" Rabia asked the driver as the cab pulled up in front of a large brick house surrounded by orange and lemon trees. It was in one of the more upscale neighborhoods in Quetta.

"It's the address you gave me."

Before Rabia could say anything further, a woman came running out of the house. "Ayeesha!" she called, swallowing Mama in a hug.

"It's all right," Rabia told the driver. She paid him and he drove away.

She barely recognized Aunt Roxanne, who had lost weight; her hair was almost completely gray. Auntie released Mama from her embrace, and fixed her gaze on Karim, who stood off to one side. Mama said something to her sister in a low voice.

"Karim, my darling." Aunt Roxanne said, approaching him. She framed his face with her hands and kissed both his cheeks.

Karim looked ill at ease, but he did not pull away.

Aunt Roxanne turned her attention to Rabia, engulfing her in a hug. "Look at you, niece," she said, holding Rabia at arm's length. "You are all grown up."

"I turned fourteen two months ago," Rabia said.

"And where is Amir?" Auntie asked, as if it had just occurred to her that he was not with them.

"He had to flee," Mama said. "To Iran." She explained about his encounter with the Taliban.

"I am sorry, Ayeesha," Aunt Roxanne said. "It must be very difficult."

"Yes," Mama agreed.

Aunt Roxanne shook her head sadly. "How was your journey?"

Mama sighed wearily. "Such a long way, sister."

"Yes," Rabia nodded in agreement. "After the bus from Kabul, two days and two nights on the train from the border to Quetta. The train was so slow, I probably could have walked here faster." She shrugged. "But…we are here now."

"I am glad to see you, niece." Aunt Roxanne said. "Your cousin, Sima, is resting, but you will see her later."

Rabia looked around the courtyard at the rosebushes

and mulberry trees. "Do you and Sima live alone here, Auntie?"

Her aunt gave a small, mirthless laugh. "Heavens no, child. We are merely servants here. I should have explained in my letter. The house belongs to Abdullah Hekmatyar and his wife, Nadia. The family owns a number of businesses in Pakistan."

"Will they mind us staying here?"

"Come inside, niece, and we will talk."

Rabia felt uneasy as they followed Aunt Roxanne into a large foyer with marble tiles. Two little boys stared, wide-eyed, as they passed. In another room, they could hear the sound of a television. Laughter floated out from behind the closed door.

Auntie led them down a wide hallway and into a dining area where a woman sat at a table with a fat baby in her arms. The woman's dark eyes studied them intently.

Introductions were made all around.

"So this is your sister and her family." Nadia Hekmatyar seemed pleased to see them. She went on to explain that their servant, Abia, was in Peshawar attending to her dying father. "And we had to fire the lazy, ungrateful Safa. All day long she watched American programs on television."

Rabia turned to look at Aunt Roxanne. Why was the woman telling them this?

"My husband is away a lot of the time," Nadia continued. "And I am busy attending to our businesses." She looked at Mama. "Our six children need constant care. Since your sister started sewing for our shops, she does not have a lot of free time to attend to household chores."

Rabia finally understood. Nadia wanted them to work for her. She must have discussed it with Aunt Roxanne before they came.

"There is a lot of work to be done in a house this size." Nadia moved the baby from her lap to her shoulder. "Meals have to be prepared. There is washing and ironing to be done. Beds to be made. In exchange, you will get room and board."

Rabia nodded numbly.

Nadia shifted her gaze from Mama to Karim, who was staring at the tiled floor. "What is wrong with the boy?" she asked bluntly.

"He has not been himself since his brother was killed," Mama said sadly.

Nadia frowned. "He will not cause trouble, will he?"

"No," Rabia said quickly. "Karim is no trouble. He is a good boy."

At that moment, a girl about Rabia's age came into the room. At first Rabia thought it might be Sima, but she quickly realized this girl was much shorter than her cousin.

"Hada," Nadia said, "bring our visitors something to eat. They must be hungry after their long journey."

The girl turned to glare at them, but did as she was told.

The baby started to fuss and Nadia stood up. "I must get this little one to bed." She fixed her gaze on Mama. "Make yourself at home. Your sister will show you to your room."

Hada returned a few minutes later carrying a platter filled with rice, chicken, lentils, chickpeas, and beans. She placed it on the table in front of them. For the next few minutes there was very little talk. They concentrated on filling their hollow bellies. It was a simple meal, but after days of nothing but naan and tea, it felt like a feast.

After they finished eating, they gathered in Aunt Roxanne and Sima's basement room. In contrast to the upstairs rooms, it was dark and dank and smelled of mold. Little light came through the high, small, rectangular windows, and the concrete walls made it feel like a dungeon. But Rabia, relaxed from the meal, did not mind. They had food, a place to stay. Even when Sima told her that she would be expected to work very hard, she was not discouraged. *It is only temporary,* she told herself. And she was overjoyed at seeing her aunt and cousin again. She had not seen them in many years, and at sixteen, Sima had grown up.

For hours, they talked about friends and relatives back in Afghanistan, Aunt Roxanne dabbing at her eyes when she learned that one of them had died. After a while, she turned her attention to Sima. My daughter is getting married," she said happily. "She is marrying Hasan the butcher."

Two bright red spots appeared in Sima's cheeks.

"I am happy for you, cousin," Rabia said, giving her a hug. "Will you and your new husband be going to America?"

Aunt Roxanne shook her head. "We have changed our minds, niece."

Rabia sucked in her breath. Had she heard right? Aunt Roxanne and Sima were not going to America?

"As it turns out, the relief organization I told you about is a Christian one. They will force us to eat pork. We will not be able to practice our Muslim faith." Aunt Roxanne lowered her voice. "There are rumors that they are taking widows and children to America to sell them into slavery."

"Auntie, where did you hear such things?" Rabia asked. She'd asked Omar to check out the organization, and, from what he learned, it rescued refugees from desperate situations around the world. Still, hearing her aunt's words unsettled her.

Chapter 6
July 2001

"Nadia and her family have decided to stay another day with their relatives," Aunt Roxanne announced at the breakfast table one morning. "They will return tomorrow."

Well, at least we will not have the bossy Hada looking over our shoulders while we work, Rabia thought. She had been in the Hekmatyar household for nearly a month now. Sima had not been mistaken when she said the work was hard. Every morning they got up at dawn, before the mullah chanted the *aazan*, the morning call to prayer. Afterwards, Hada and her brothers and sisters went back to bed. Rabia and Sima stayed awake to help Mama and Aunt Roxanne with the housework. They were kept busy every minute of the day — cleaning, cooking, scrubbing floors, doing laundry and other chores. At the end of the day her arms and back ached from all the heavy lifting. Hada, who was only a year older than Rabia, ordered the girls around like slaves.

Despite all of this, Aunt Roxanne had decided not to go to America. And now, she had Mama convinced that bad things would happen. Rumors were running wild in Quetta that refugees would be sold into slavery. Mama was terrified, and Rabia was afraid she might change her mind about going.

Rabia pushed eggs around on her plate. She could not imagine spending her life here working for this family. The only thing that made it bearable was having her cousin beside her. She and Sima had grown close during their time together. *It will not be too long now, before I can leave*, Rabia reminded herself. In a few days, the relief organization would be setting up its headquarters. Nadia had grudgingly said Rabia could go to register. Mama though, would have to stay behind to help with the housework.

"Nadia wants the children's playroom cleaned before they return," Aunt Roxanne said, yanking Rabia out of her thoughts. "You girls can start right after breakfast. Ayeesha and I will take care of the breakfast dishes."

Sima got up from the table. "We might as well get started," she said.

Rabia took her dishes to the sink and followed Sima down the wide hallway to the playroom. "What a mess," Sima said when she opened the door.

Rabia glanced around the room. Stuffed animals, books, dolls, toy trucks and cars littered the carpet. The room had high ceilings and was painted a bright yellow. Two large windows looked out on a well-tended lawn. There were shelves filled with books and toys. A desk held a computer with all the latest games and software. "Nadia should make her children clean up after themselves," Sima said. "They are like little pigs."

Rabia had never seen so many toys and games. Nadia's children were very spoiled. And they were unruly at times. She let her eyes stray to the corner of the room where a large television with a VCR stood on a shelf. Maybe they could watch a program while they worked. Rarely did they get to watch television, they were kept so busy with household chores.

An idea suddenly came to Rabia. "I will be right back," she told Sima and quickly left the room. She returned minutes later holding the video. She removed it from its plastic case, and slipped it into the VCR.

Sima watched the screen, a confused look on her face. After some time a black-and-white image of a large ship emerged. Crowds of people waved from the deck. Sima continued to watch, not knowing what to expect.

Then suddenly the image changed to a dark rolling sea and the single word *TITANIC* appeared on the screen.

"Rabia?" Sima asked breathlessly. "Where did you get this movie?"

"I brought it with me," Rabia said, pleased with herself. The look on her cousin's face was worth the risk she had taken smuggling it out of Afghanistan. "I thought we could watch it while we cleaned."

Several minutes went by without either of them lifting a finger. They were too absorbed in what was happening on the screen. Finally, Rabia picked up a dust rag. "We better get this place cleaned up," she said.

Sima began picking up toys and books, her eyes glued to the television set.

From the beginning, their hearts were with the two main characters, Rose and Jack. They laughed out loud when Jack taught Rose to fly on the bow of the boat. They clapped when Rose defied her mother by choosing Jack over the rich Cal Hockley, to whom she had been promised in marriage. They shot each other nervous glances when the ship hit an iceberg.

An hour later, Rabia left the room to get a fresh pail of water.

"You girls are taking a long time cleaning the playroom," Aunt Roxanne said.

"It is very dirty, Auntie," Rabia said, feeling guilty

for deceiving her aunt. But Mama and Aunt Roxanne were sitting at the kitchen table drinking tea. They did not seem to be in any hurry to clean the house. *Good for them,* Rabia thought. *They deserve a little free time after working like dogs all week long.*

When Rabia returned to the playroom, Sima was sitting on the floor crying, her hands covering her face.

"Cousin, it is only a film," Rabia said. "A true story, yes. But it happened so long ago, the people would all be dead now."

"It's not that," Sima sniffed.

"Then what is it?" Rabia knelt on the floor beside her. "Are you okay?"

Sima swiped at her eyes. "If only I had the courage to stand up to Mama the way Rose stood up to *her* mother."

Rabia put a hand on her cousin's shoulder. "What are you saying, Sima?"

"I don't want to marry Hasan," Sima admitted. She looked at Rabia with such sorrow, it broke her heart.

"Did you tell your mother how you feel?"

"Mama thinks that if I don't marry Hasan, I will not find another husband." She met Rabia's gaze. "She's concerned about what will happen to me when she is no longer around. That is part of the reason she did not want to go to America. She didn't want me to leave Hasan."

Sima bit her lip. "Hasan and his family were born here and have no desire to leave."

Rabia stared silently at her cousin.

"If I marry Hasan, I will be trapped forever," Sima continued. "I do not want to get married. Not to Hasan, not to anyone. I want to go to America." She grasped Rabia's arm. "You are so lucky, Rabia. In America, girls are free to choose whom they want to marry. And if they do not wish to marry, no one cares. Your life is so full of hope, while mine is..." Fresh tears spilled down Sima's cheeks.

Rabia didn't know what to say. She glanced helplessly at the television screen where the *Titanic* was filling up with water. Panic-stricken passengers were screaming and shouting, all trying desperately to get away from the doomed ship.

Chapter 7
September 11, 2001

We're leaving, Rabia wanted to shout as the plane picked up speed, the gray tarmac rushing past the window. After months of waiting, it was finally happening. She was on her way to America. On her way to a better life where she had a chance to go to school, go to college if she chose. Even so, as the plane climbed and banked, Islamabad tilting beneath her, she felt a small twinge of regret. She was leaving behind friends and relatives, everything familiar. Would she ever see Father and Amir again?

She glanced at Karim; he was staring straight ahead, his expression hard to read. Mama's eyes were red from weeping. *It is going to be okay, Mama,* Rabia wanted to reassure her. *Things will be better in America. You can be a photographer again. Maybe even have your own studio.*

Rabia could only imagine what her mother was going through. Not only was she uncertain about going to America, but Mama also felt guilty about leaving Father and Amir behind. Rabia had tried to convince her that she was not abandoning her husband and son. This move was good for all of them. Hadn't Father prepared his children for the day when they would possibly go to America? In Afghanistan they were shut in the house most of the time, afraid to go out. In Pakistan, they would always be refugees and servants.

Mama will grow to love America, Rabia told herself. She only wished Sima could have come with them. *Dear, sweet Sima, you deserve to be happy. I can only pray that you will find the courage to stand up to Aunt Roxanne,* Rabia thought as she gazed out the window at the shrinking mountains and blue-domed mosques of Pakistan.

Making it into the program had been much more difficult than Rabia had imagined. The relief organization had set up their operation on an isolated field outside Quetta where thousands of refugees flocked to register. For three days, Rabia tried to obtain an interview. The first couple of days she couldn't get anywhere near the gate.

In the end, it was her foot that saved her. Rabia smiled now at the memory. Not that her artificial foot made her stand out in any way. Hundreds of people who came to register had missing limbs. Many of them were worse off than she.

After days of waiting, people had grown frustrated. They pushed and shoved, elbowing their way to the gates. Rabia was jostled from side to side. She stumbled, and, to her horror, her prosthesis fell off. Losing her balance, she landed flat on her face. She might have been trampled if a man from the organization hadn't picked her up. He ushered her inside the gate, gave her a glass of water and a bandage for her scraped forehead. For hours she waited on a wooden bench, her head throbbing and her leg aching. But Rabia didn't mind. She was finally going to be interviewed. Her family would have a chance to go to America.

Rabia turned her attention to the brochure she had been given. She felt a surge of excitement as she looked at the colorful photographs of California, the state they were going to. Rows of wood and brick houses ran along wide tree-lined avenues. Tall glass buildings rose into the sky. The lady at the relief office told her that California was more than seven thousand miles from Afghanistan. *Seven thousand miles to freedom,* Rabia thought.

In America, people shopped at places called malls that had dozens of stores and moving staircases. A woman from the organization told her that in a mall you could buy everything from bread and books to television sets and clothing.

There were photographs of women and men walking along white sandy beaches. The women wore scanty clothing. Rabia knew she could never walk around half naked like that. But she would never again hide her face under a burqa. She turned a page in the brochure, pausing to look at a picture of a girl running down a grassy knoll, long hair streaming in the wind. She tried to imagine her own long dark hair flying free. Leaning back in her seat, Rabia felt the powerful thrust of the engine carry her upward into the clouds.

Chapter 8
September 11, 2001 — London, England

Colin stood by the airport gift shop, glancing up at a television suspended from the ceiling. It was tuned to a CNN news channel. From nearby he could hear his mother and grandmother talking. "He hasn't called once since we've been here," Mom was saying.

Colin cocked his head in their direction. His mother was talking about his dad.

"Maybe it isn't possible for him to call," Grandma said. "William travels so much with his job."

"True," Mom agreed. "Still, it's hard on Colin not having a father in his life. He'll be twelve in a couple of weeks, and he hardly knows Will."

Colin bit his lip. How could Mom know how he felt? Whenever he tried to talk to her about Dad, she changed the subject.

"It's hard on you too, dear." Grandma's voice was gentle.

"I didn't realize it would be this bad," Mom said. "We can't go on like this."

Does Mom want a divorce? Colin wondered, feeling his pulse quicken. He recalled a fight his parents had earlier in the summer. Through the closed door of his bedroom, he had listened to their raised, angry voices. "I've spent years building up a law practice," Mom said. "Do you expect me to throw it all away to follow you to some godforsaken part of the globe?"

Please don't fight, Colin had begged silently. He hated it when his parents argued, and they were doing it more and more these days. Dad's work as a diplomat took him all over the world. Now he was posted in Kenya, and he wanted his family to go with him. Mom didn't take the news well.

Colin turned back to the television set. A man with glasses and a white beard was reporting on a baby who'd been left alone in an apartment in Manhattan. As news cameras scanned the familiar landmarks, Colin felt the ache of homesickness. *I'll be back in New York soon,* he reminded himself.

"Colin?" Grandma came to stand beside him. "I've enjoyed our visit so much."

"Thank you for everything, Grandma," Colin

replied. "I had a swell time."

And he meant it. During his stay, Grandma had taken him to the Tower of London and to Buckingham Palace to watch the Changing of the Guard. Yesterday, they'd taken a bus to visit Dover Castle. From the turrets, they saw clear across the English Channel to France. But now he was more than ready to go home. School had already started, and he was looking forward to seeing his friends again. He missed his dog, Jake, who was staying with his best friend, Grant, while he and Mom were away.

"When you get home, try to get your mom to go to her yoga sessions." Grandma glanced quickly toward an information booth where Mom was talking with an agent. "It will do wonders for her headaches." She frowned. "I'm quite concerned about Catherine's headaches."

"It's stress." Colin shrugged. "At least, that's what she says."

"All the more reason she should practice yoga. And tai chi is another marvelous exercise."

"I'll try to convince her," Colin promised.

Grandma reached into her bag and pulled out a brightly wrapped gift. "I got you a little something."

"But Grandma, you already gave me my birthday gift."

"This is to celebrate going into sixth grade."

Colin grinned. Grandma could find a reason to celebrate almost anything. "Thanks," he said, accepting the gift. He tore off the wrapping. It was a book: *The Young Person's Odyssey.*

"It's a retelling of Homer's epic poem," Grandma said. "I used to read it over and over when I was your age. I hope you'll get as much pleasure from it as I did."

Colin doubted that, but he hugged his grandmother. "Thanks Grandma. I'll read it on the plane."

Catherine was making her way toward them. "We should head for customs," she said, glancing at her watch. She hugged Grandma. "Thanks for everything, Mother. I'll call you when we get home."

"And thanks again for the book," Colin said.

Grandma kissed his cheek. "Be sure to write me now and then. I'll miss you."

While they waited to board the plane, Colin got out the electronic game he'd brought from home. He hadn't played it much at Grandma's house because she thought it was too violent. The object was to blow up space aliens. If he got a hundred in sixty seconds, he could go on to the next level. Colin shook his head. You'd think he was killing real people the way Grandma carried on.

As he watched the screen light up, Colin thought of the conversation he'd heard earlier between his mother and grandmother. A heavy feeling settled in his stomach. Things were not going well between Mom and Dad. Two aliens appeared on the screen. He blew them away.

. . .

The plane was nearly full when Colin and his mother boarded and found their seats. Colin looked around at the other passengers. The plane had come from Pakistan. Across the aisle from them sat a woman with two children, a boy and a girl. *They don't look like people on vacation,* he thought. Their clothing was faded and threadbare, and they were thin, like the starving people he had seen on television. The mother's face was sad and pinched. The little boy had a stunned look, as if someone had startled him. The girl, who was about his own age, looked more serious than any kid he'd ever seen. Her dark eyes were too big for her thin, grave face. She saw Colin looking at her, and flashed him a shy smile. He returned the smile, and gave her a thumbs up before turning on his electronic game.

Colin was so absorbed in trying to get to the fourth level of the game, he barely noticed when the plane took off. "Yes!" he shouted as he worked the controls. Arms, legs, and heads exploded on the small screen. With satisfaction, he watched as one icon after another was blown to bits. He heard nothing but the beep-beeping of the gadget. "Yes! Another one bites the dust."

After a while the beeps became faint, until finally the game stopped. "Oh no," Colin groaned. "The batteries!" He turned to his mother.

"Well, you've been playing the thing since we left London."

Darn! Colin thought. Why hadn't he remembered to bring an extra set? "What do I do now?"

Mom reached into his backpack, pulled out the book Grandma had given him. "Read," she said.

Colin made a face. The last thing he wanted to do was read, but he took the book and flipped it open. *Looks interesting enough,* he thought, gazing at the colorful illustrations of one-eyed monsters and other strange creatures.

Even before he'd read the prologue — before Odysseus began his journey — Colin was hooked. He loved how Odysseus tricked the Trojans. For ten years the Greeks had tried to fight their way into Troy. But the walls were strong, and the Trojans were great warriors. Odysseus's plan took them completely by surprise. Pretending to surrender, the Greeks boarded their ships and sailed out of sight. On the beach, they left a large wooden horse with armed warriors hidden inside. The Trojans, thinking it was an offering to Poseidon, dragged the horse through the gates of the city. That night, warriors crawled out of the horse's belly, killed the guards, and opened the gates to the Greek soldiers who had been anchored in the harbor, waiting. But as Odysseus fled the burning city, Poseidon's anger was stirred. He set the tides and winds against Odysseus, and summoned all the monsters of the sea.

Colin was so engaged in the story he didn't even stop reading when the captain's voice boomed over the intercom. He only looked up from the book when he heard the words *national emergency.*

"Airspace over the United States is closed," the captain announced. "We will be landing at an airport in Gander, Newfoundland, in approximately thirty minutes."

There was a moment of stunned silence, followed by gasps of surprise from the passengers.

"Airspace over the United States is closed," repeated a man a few aisles over. "That's never happened before."

Colin put down his book, feeling uneasy. Were they being hijacked? Was that why they couldn't go home to New York?

His mother squeezed his shoulder.

"Where in the world is Newfoundland?" a passenger asked.

"Never heard of it," a lady's voice piped up.

"It's a province in Canada." Catherine took a map from her bag and spread it on her lap. "Right here," she said, talking more to herself than to the people around her. She tapped a fingernail on a large triangular island in the Atlantic Ocean. "In fact," she said, turning to Colin. "Aunt Bea's from Newfoundland."

"Aunt Bea?" Uncle Henry had met Aunt Bea during the war. Colin thought she was as crazy as a bat. She spoke with an odd accent and called everyone my dear, or my love. Whenever Mom and Colin went to visit them in Florida, she cooked strange food — fish and brewis, figgy duff, and lassie buns.

"Well," Colin said, trying to keep his voice light, "maybe we'll get to have fried cod tongues again." But even as he spoke, he couldn't ignore the frantic thoughts fluttering through his mind like trapped moths. Something was terribly wrong.

Chapter 9
Gander, Newfoundland

"All students are to clean out their desks," the principal's voice rumbled over the PA system at Gander Academy. "All textbooks, papers, pens, and notebooks must be taken with you when you leave today."

Leah Pickford glanced at the clock on the classroom wall. There were still twenty minutes before classes ended.

"Don't leave *anything* behind," the principal continued. "And another thing…" He paused as a plane roared overhead. "All classes are cancelled tomorrow."

This announcement was greeted by a chorus of cheers from Miss Pelly's sixth grade students.

Leah watched kids stuff notebooks and papers into their knapsacks. She looked at the large calendar near the blackboard. Tomorrow was Wednesday, September 12. It wasn't a holiday. There wouldn't be any in-service days until October; Miss Pelly had said so. Why then, were they closing school in the middle of the week? Something wasn't right. She raised her hand.

"Yes, Leah?"

"Why is school closed tomorrow?"

Other students had their eyes fixed on the teacher.

"There's been a…um…situation in the United States. Some planes have been diverted. Passengers will be using our school as a shelter."

"You're kidding, right?" Kyle Elliott said. He looked around. "People are actually going to sleep in here? What's wrong with the motels?"

Leah was wondering the same thing. Gander was a small town, but it had a number of fine hotels. "What kind of a situation?" she asked, warily.

"Well, I suppose you'll find out soon enough," the teacher said. "There's been an attack on the United States. Planes hijacked by terrorists flew into the twin towers of the World Trade Center. All airports in the U.S. are shut down."

"But—"

Miss Pelley shrugged. "That's all I know." She looked toward the open window. "Go home," she said. "Enjoy this beautiful weather while it lasts. We're not going to get many more fall days like this one."

An attack, Leah thought as she walked home. It sounded serious. Did this mean war? She felt the familiar stabbing pain in her stomach. No doubt, her ulcer was acting up again. She could hear Granny's voice in her head. "You worries too much, my love. Lets every little thing get to you."

Doc Drover had said the same thing. She remembered the frown on his face when her test results came back. "A girl your age shouldn't have an ulcer," he told her. He had asked her to wait in the examination room so he could talk alone with Aunt Flo in his office. Leah did as she was asked, but heard every word they said through the thin wall that separated the two rooms. She felt a flush of embarrassment now, remembering the way they talked about her.

"She's always been a very sensitive, high strung child," Aunt Flo told the doctor. "Worries about everything. And it's got worse since her father died."

"How long will her mother be away?"

"Debbie's got another ten months 'til she finishes her nursing program," Aunt Flo replied. "I told her the youngsters could stay as long as they needs to. I helped raise Debbie; she's more like a daughter than a niece. Sure, Leah and Brent is like me own grandchildren."

"What about the boy?" Doc asked. "How has all this affected him?"

"Brent?" Aunt Flo gave a short laugh. "Nothing bothers that one. The house could fall down on his head and he wouldn't even notice. I've never seen two youngsters so different."

It was true. Leah shifted her heavy backpack from one shoulder to the other. Nothing seemed to faze her nine-year-old brother. "A ball of energy," Mom called him. Leah glanced at her watch. If she hurried, she might catch the beginning of *General Hospital*. Since the bus drivers went on strike, she'd been walking home, and sometimes the program was half over by the time she got there.

Granny sat at the table, a cigarette burning in the ashtray beside her. A wreath of smoke circled her head. "You're out of school early," she said.

Leah told her about the attack on the United States.

Granny nodded. "I know. It's all over the news." She shook her head. "There's an ill wind that don't blow someone good."

"Is Aunt Flo working late?"

Granny glanced at the clock on the kitchen wall. "She should be home soon. Eli called to say he'll be late."

At that moment, Brent burst through the door, his coat torn, red hair sticking from beneath his cap. "Granny! Granny, you'll never guess what happened."

"Slow down, child."

Brent paused to catch his breath. "Guy Fawkes went and blowed up two big buildings in New York."

"G'wan with yeh, Brent." Granny laughed. "Guy Fawkes has been dead for hundreds of years."

"And oh my, Granny," Brent went on as if she hadn't spoken. "Thousands of planes coming in to the airport. Jason's dad is taking him to see all the jumbo jets. Can I go with them, Granny? Can I?"

Smiling, Leah shook her head. She walked down the hall to her bedroom and tossed the knapsack onto her bed. The room was small with barely enough space for a narrow bed and chest of drawers. Uncle Eli had built a shelf on the wall for a small television. She turned it on. The screen flickered to life showing two tall buildings, fire and smoke billowing from the sides. The twin towers of the World Trade Center, she realized. With trembling hands, she turned up the sound. "It is estimated that thousands are dead and thousands more injured," a journalist said.

Leah watched as one of the buildings plummeted to the ground. Her stomach churned, making her queasy. She switched to another channel, and watched a replay of the second tower collapsing. "Hundreds jumped to their deaths when the towers fell this morning," the reporter said.

This is bad, Leah thought. She flicked from channel to channel, watching as the towers fell again and again.

Chapter 10

Colin noticed the girl across the aisle looking his way, her gaze troubled. *She's worried,* he thought. He flashed what he hoped was a reassuring smile, although he had no clue what was going on himself.

Colin turned to his mother. "Mom, what do you suppose is happening?"

His mother closed her eyes. "I don't know, Colin. I already told you that."

Colin picked up his book. No use talking to Mom when she had one of her headaches. In the hours since they'd landed at Gander, he'd heard scraps of information. There were rumors that the plane had been hijacked, that the hijackers and the police were working out a deal. They were saying that all over the United States, planes were being hijacked and flown into buildings. Mom had tried to use her cell phone to call home, but was unable to make a connection. She got a Canadian operator who told her that all lines to the U.S. were blocked.

Colin tried to concentrate on his book. When the captain made his announcement, he had just finished reading about how Odysseus's son, Telemachus, left in the night to go in search of his father. Now, he was at the part in the story where Odysseus and his men arrived on the island of Aeolid, home of Aelus, guardian of the wind. Aelus and his family welcomed the visitors with kindness and hospitality. Everyday was a holiday on the island, with banquets, feasting, and much gaiety.

Darkness was falling by the time a set of portable steps was brought to the door of the plane. "Thank God," Catherine said. "Finally we can disembark." She picked up her purse from under the seat. Colin got his knapsack from the overhead compartment.

"Are we going to a hotel?" he asked as they followed a line of passengers across the tarmac to customs and immigration.

"I don't know," his mother answered, wearily. "We may have to sleep in the airport."

At customs, a man scanned them with a metal detector. Their carry-on luggage was opened and searched. Colin watched as his mom's makeup, fingernail polish, wallet, and appointment book tumbled out.

A woman with a clipboard directed them down a long hallway. As they turned the corner, Colin saw men and women in red-and-white vests. He knew they were from the Red Cross because last year, volunteers had come to his school to talk about how they helped victims of earthquakes, floods, and other disasters. Colin pulled his mother's sleeve. "Why do we need the Red Cross?" he whispered, feeling a rush of panic.

Mom didn't answer.

A volunteer handed them each a bag containing a sandwich and bottle of water.

Gratefully, Colin accepted the food. Were they victims of a disaster now? Would they ever be able to go back home to New York? A lump rose in his throat, nearly choking him.

Women hurried by with sleeping babies and crying children. So many people: men wearing turbans, women in burqas and headscarves. All around them, people spoke in languages Colin didn't understand. Everyone looked tired and frightened.

The people at the desks and luggage counters had accents like Aunt Bea, and they kept talking about someone named Buddy.

"Buddy over there will take care of you, look."

"Tell Buddy he forgot his passport."

"Go see Buddy, he'll fix you up."

The woman with the clipboard led them outside where rows of school buses lined the parking lot. A number of local volunteers stood by ready to help. "They're taking the passengers to a shelter," one of them explained.

Shelter? But shelters are for animals and homeless people, aren't they? Colin turned to his mother. She looked ready to keel over.

One of the volunteers must have thought the same thing. She came to Catherine and gently touched her shoulder. "You okay, my dear?"

"Headache," Catherine mumbled.

"Oh, my dear. Must be terrible traveling with a bad head." The woman glanced at her clipboard. "Passengers from your flight are being bussed to Gambo," she said. "That's about a half-hour drive from here." She put a hand on Catherine's arm. "Tell you what. Since you're not feeling well, I'll put you on a bus to the Gander Academy."

Gander Academy? They were going to a school?

"Thank you," Catherine whispered gratefully. "I just need to lie down."

The woman led them to one of the busses. After a word with the driver, she motioned for Colin and his mother to get on. Catherine sagged down in her seat, rested her head against the window, and closed her eyes. Colin stared out into the darkness.

More volunteers met them at the school. A table with juice packs and bottles of water was set up in the foyer. No sooner were they inside than a woman approached. The nametag stuck on her sweater said Jennifer. "You the lady with the bad head?" she asked. "I got a call from the airport."

Catherine nodded.

"Follow me," she said, leading them down a long hallway. "I'll put you both in one of the smaller classrooms where it's quieter."

Through open doors, Colin saw air mattresses and sleeping bags scattered across classroom floors. They followed Jennifer to the end of the corridor. She opened the door of a small classroom. All the overhead lights had been turned off except for one near the door. "This is where you'll sleep," she said, ushering them inside.

Glancing around the dim room, Colin saw that desks had been shoved against the wall to make room for cots and mattresses.

"There are four other families in here," Jennifer said. "All women with children."

Although it was only a little past nine o'clock, the families were already bedded down for the night. Jennifer led them to a cot in the corner of the room. Beside it was a mattress. "You take the mattress," Catherine told Colin. "I'll take the cot." She kicked off her shoes.

Jennifer handed them blankets. "Not the Hilton," she said, almost apologetically, "but there won't be any more people sharing this room. I'll turn out the light."

"Thank you," Catherine muttered.

Colin lay on the mattress. Despite his weariness, he couldn't fall asleep. Troubled thoughts tumbled through his head. It was a long time before he finally drifted off.

Chapter 11

Rabia glanced around the large room at the molded plastic chairs and pale green walls. After going through customs, they had been brought here by a woman named Emma. "Someone will come for you shortly, Ray-bia," she said, pronouncing her name, incorrectly.

"*Rah-bee-ah*," she corrected silently. *My name is Rah-bee-ah*, but she smiled and nodded politely at the woman. The woman smiled back.

"Where will they take us?" Rabia asked, feeling a stab of anxiety.

The woman shrugged.

There were about a dozen other people in the room, most of them old. Some were in wheelchairs. An elderly man coughed into a handkerchief.

Why did they bring us here? Rabia wondered, feeling

her heart flutter with panic. *Why?* Rabia heard someone say that the United States was under attack. What did that mean? If America *had* been attacked, would they still be able to go there, or would they be put on a plane back to Pakistan? They were not citizens of Pakistan and didn't have passports. Even worse, if they were returned to Afghanistan, it would be the end of them.

"Gander, Newfoundland," Rabia whispered. *How far are we from California?* she wondered. *How many more miles to freedom?*

If only she could find a phone, she would call Fatima, her caseworker at the relief organization. She might know something. Fatima had given Rabia her number and told her to call if there was a problem. Rabia had passed a bank of payphones when she came through customs. All had signs on them and a man stood, motioning people to keep moving. He kept repeating "Out of order."

A girl came into the room and took a seat across from Rabia. She stared in disbelief at the sight of her. Her hair was orange and green like a parrot, and stood up in spikes. Surely no one was born with hair like that. The girl wore baggy shorts and a shirt that came down to her knees. She took an object from her pocket and began punching it with her fingers. She put it to her ear. A wireless phone, Rabia realized. She had heard of such things.

Rabia listened with interest to the conversation.

"He goes, 'Why did you dye the dog purple?' And I'm like, 'It's my dog and I'll dye him any color I want.' And he's like, 'That's puppy abuse.' And I'm like, 'Well, if you're so concerned, why don't you call the SPCA?' And he goes… 'Well, you know they won't do anything.' And I'm like…'Well, duh….'"

What a strange conversation, Rabia thought.

"I'll call you back, Brittany," the girl said. She glared at Rabia. "What?" she said, folding the phone.

"What has happened?" Rabia asked. "Why are we being held here?"

"How would I know?" Scowling, the girl turned her back on Rabia.

What a strange, rude girl, Rabia thought. *Probably she is American and upset because her country is under attack.*

Rabia stretched out her leg, wincing from the throbbing ache where her prosthesis was attached. She needed a new one; this one was cracked in places and no longer fit properly.

Emma returned to the room followed by a young couple. "Jim and Daisy Hayes," she called, looking around.

An elderly man stood up. "That's us, Daisy," he said. "C'mon, dear." He reached for his wife's arm.

"This is Adam and Darlene House," Emma told them. "They're going to take you to their home." Rabia watched them shake hands and follow the couple out the door. *Is that what we are waiting for — someone to take us home?* Rabia wondered. Then another sobering thought jumped into her mind. *What if no one comes for us?*

Rabia needed to go to the toilet. Maybe Emma could show her where it was. She stood up and walked toward her. "I need go…" She could not remember the English word. Sometimes when she didn't know the English, she would mime what she meant, but not this time. She felt her cheeks flush.

"Do you need to go to the bathroom?" Emma asked.

Bathroom. Yes, that was it. Rabia nodded gratefully.

"Come, I'll show you where it is."

The bathroom was large and bright with beige and brown wall tiles. A mirror ran the length of the wall. Rabia counted six sinks, all with gleaming silver faucets. She leaned toward the mirror and studied her reflection. There were dark smudges beneath her eyes, and her face looked thin and haggard.

Rabia was in one of the stalls when she heard two women come into the room.

"Imagine, killing thousands of innocent people," one of them said.

"Some people are pure evil," the second woman replied.

"President Bush should go in there and drop a bomb. Blow them all to pieces."

There was a murmur of agreement from the other woman. "There could be terrorists on the planes for all we know."

Is that why we were kept on the runway so long after landing? Rabia wondered. She waited until the two women left, then found her way back to the waiting room, a feeling of dread growing larger with every step she took. She only knew one thing for certain: Whatever was happening was not good.

More people arrived, and more names were called from the list. Finally, a woman and young boy about Rabia's age came into the room. The woman was wearing denim pants and a checked shirt. Her dark hair was cropped so short that Rabia mistook her for a man. She had noticed that a lot of women dressed like men in this country.

"Oh, my dear, so sorry to keep everybody waiting," the woman said. "Kevin, my husband, was gone with the van. It's been so busy... what with all the..."

"This is Millie Keating," Emma cut in. "And her son, Jason. Millie's going to take you to her home." She turned her attention to Rabia's family. "And this," she said, "is the Atmar family — Rabia, Karim, and their mother, Ayeesha. They're from Afghanistan."

Millie Keating held out her hand. "So nice to meet you all."

Jason gave them a wide smile.

"Rabia," Millie said. "Now that's a name you don't hear too often. I must tell Tanya, my niece. She's having a baby," she explained, "and they've gone through dozens of baby books searching for unusual names. Can't make up their minds. They knows 'tis a girl. Had an ultrasound done weeks ago."

"Mom," Jason said. "I doubt they care." He smiled at Rabia.

"Help the girl with her luggage," Millie told him.

"Is okay," Rabia said, clutching the drawstring pouch. Everything she owned was in the bag, and she was not going to let it out of her sight.

They followed Millie and Jason to the parking lot where a minivan was parked.

"Some nice weather," Millie said. "Can't remember a fall that's been this nice."

Rabia sniffed the clean fresh air. It smelled wonderful. And there was something else. "It is so quiet."

"Quiet?" Millie gave her a puzzled look.

Rabia could hear the hum of cars on the highway, a dog barking in the distance. In Kabul, there was always the sound of gunfire. Bombs and rockets rained down regularly. During the civil war, they fell night and day, destroying buildings and killing people. Many times Rabia and her family had scurried for shelter in the middle of the night.

Jason opened the front passenger door and gestured for Ayeesha to get in. He pulled open the side door, and Rabia and Karim climbed into the back.

Millie got behind the wheel, and started the engine. "Your family will be staying in our basement apartment," she told Ayeesha, as she backed the van out of the parking lot. "Our tenant won't be moving in until the end of the month."

Mama looked confused, so Rabia translated in Dari. "Mama does not understand English very well," she explained.

"But you certainly speak very well, my dear," Millie said.

"My father. He teach me," Rabia said proudly.

"And what about your brother?" She turned her head slightly. "Karim, is it?"

"Karim...he does not talk."

"Oh." Millie said. "Oh, my!" Thankfully, she didn't ask questions, and Rabia didn't go into any detail. Instead, she stared out the window at the passing scenery.

Millie drove to a neighborhood with tidy houses

and carefully trimmed lawns. A few minutes later, she pulled the van into a circular driveway in front of a large brick house with a double garage. Jason got out and opened the passenger door for Mama. Rabia and Karim climbed out the back.

"Jason," Millie said, "could you show them to the apartment?" She turned to Rabia. You'll no doubt be needing to rest. If yeh needs anything, my love, give me a shout, okay?"

"*Tashakor*," Rabia said. "Thank you."

"This way," Jason said, leading them around the back of the house. He opened the door to a small foyer, then another to the apartment. Neither door was locked. "It's small," he said, switching on the living room light.

Rabia took in her surroundings. The room had a sofa, two chairs, and a small television on a stand. It was much bigger than the room they'd shared in Kabul.

"Sofa converts into a bed," Jason said, pulling down the back to demonstrate.

There was a kitchenette with cupboards, sink, fridge, stove, and a small table with four chairs. Jason opened the fridge. "Mom left egg sandwiches," he said. "There's cheese and fruit. Milk and sugar for tea."

"Thank you," Rabia said. She was starting to feel hungry.

"In here's the bedroom," Jason led them into a small room off the kitchen. The room had a double bed with a white ruffled spread. There was a small set of drawers, and a little table with a lamp and a telephone on it.

"Can I use this telephone?" Rabia asked. "I will make a...collect call." Fatima had told her about collect calls and how to make them in case she needed to.

"That phone doesn't work yet," Jason said. "But you can use the one upstairs. Come, I'll show you where it's to."

"I try to call at the airport," Rabia told him when they were outside. "The phones do not work."

Jason shook his head. "That's what they wants people to believe. My stepfather works at the airport. He told me they wanted to get everyone through the airport as quickly as possible. Didn't want people stopping to use the phones." He led Rabia up a set of concrete steps. "Made sure all the televisions were turned off too, they did. S'pose they thought the shock would be too much for most people."

It must be very bad, Rabia thought. "What happened?" She summoned up her courage to ask.

"You mean you don't know?"

"Yes, I hear something...an attack...."

"Terrorists flew planes into two buildings in New York. A lot of people were killed."

76

"Why do you take us to your home? Why do we not go with the others?"

Jason looked down at her prosthesis. "I s'pose it's because of your...disability. Families with elderly or disabled members are being sent to private homes."

"I am not disabled," Rabia said firmly. What did this boy know? He had not seen her play soccer. Before the Taliban came with their silly rules, she had played soccer all the time and kept up with the others.

Jason shrugged. "Be thankful you don't have to stay at a shelter. The apartment's small, but at least you'll have privacy."

The boy was right, Rabia realized. Crowds frightened Karim. "Thank you," she said. "Your family is kind."

Jason nodded, absently. "What happened to your foot?"

"In Afghanistan, I stepped on landmine."

"Geez." Jason frowned. He opened the screen door and led her through a large foyer into a well-furnished room. The walls were painted a soft gray and the wooden floors gleamed. A large painting of the ocean hung over the fireplace.

"Phone's in there." Jason gestured toward a small kitchen where a phone hung on the wall.

There were no people around, but Rabia heard

a buzz of conversation coming from one of the other rooms. She dialed the operator and gave her Fatima's number, exactly the way she had been instructed. The phone rang twice before a recording cut in. *All circuits to the United States are busy.* Sighing, Rabia hung up.

• • •

Rabia knelt in front of the television. An image of Osama bin Laden filled the screen. He was wearing his military uniform and holding a rifle. Mama looked questioningly at Rabia. The picture changed to a panel of reporters. "It appears that bin Laden was behind the attacks," one of them said.

Rabia sucked in her breath. As she listened, she became more and more disturbed. "Bin Laden and his followers see this as a religious war between Islam and America," she translated for Mama.

"People have been murdered in the name of Islam?" Mama's dark eyes flashed, and for a moment she seemed like her old self. "Osama bin Laden has made a mockery of our faith. Made a mockery of all that is good and holy."

Rabia nodded, uneasily.

Mama turned from the television and went to the stove to pour tea.

Rabia moved to the sofa, her eyes riveted on the television. A reporter was talking to a man in a blue suit. Words crawled across the bottom of the screen. On a split screen, Rabia could see the devastation left by the destruction of the towers. Smoke still rose from the site. It reminded her of the bombings in Kabul.

"Do you think there will be a backlash against Muslims because of this?" the reporter asked.

Rabia turned up the sound, her heart skipping beats.

"It's hard to know just how people will react," the man in the blue suit replied. "Of course, we all remember what happened after the attack on Pearl Harbor. Japanese Americans were rounded up and put in prison."

Rabia stared at the television.

"No," she whispered quietly.

Chapter 12

"Eli says they're expecting about seven thousand passengers," Aunt Flo told her friend over the phone. "Don't know how we're going to handle them all." She held the receiver in one hand while putting chopped onion into a pot with the other. "Some of the local restaurants are donating food. The grocery store is going to stay open all night in case anyone needs anything."

Leah shook her head, amused. Aunt Flo hadn't stopped since she'd come home from the department store where she worked as a cashier. As soon as she'd heard about the diverted planes, she clicked into high gear. She'd made a batch of potato salad and a platter of ham and cheese sandwiches. She had gone to the grocery store to pick up a roast and a chicken. Two pots of soup simmered on the stove. Earlier, she had canvassed the neighborhood collecting clothes and bedding for the stranded passengers.

"Well, Millie girl, I gotta run," she said. "There's still lots to do. I'll see you tomorrow at the school." Aunt Flo hung up the phone and turned to Leah. "Leah, my love, did you peel them eggs like I asked?"

"I put them in the fridge, Aunt Flo."

"Thanks, my love. I'm going to go through the linen closet — look for extra sheets and bedding. Will yeh check the oven for me from time to time?"

"Sure." Leah went into the living room where Granny was sorting through bags of clothing.

A few minutes later, Eli arrived home. He was Mom's brother, and Aunt Flo's nephew. He had moved in with Aunt Flo a couple of weeks ago after being burned out of his apartment. He sank down in a chair, exhausted. "I never want to see another air mattress so long as I lives."

"You okay, my dear?" Granny asked. "You looks like something that got chewed up and spit out."

"And I feels like it, too." Uncle Eli ran his fingers through his unruly sandy hair.

"Did yeh have supper?"

"They were handing out pizza to the volunteers."

Granny made a face. "Leah," she said. "Get Eli some decent food."

Leah went into the kitchen, and ladled up stew

from the pot at the back of the stove. She cut off a piece of bread and buttered it.

"See any movie stars, Uncle Eli?" Brent asked.

"No stars out tonight, Brent."

Leah rolled her eyes. Brent could be so lame. He asked the same question every evening. Uncle Eli worked as a baggage checker at the airport. Shortly after he'd moved in, he told Brent about seeing Oprah Winfrey, Brad Pitt, and other celebrities who stopped at the airport. Now, apparently Brent thought celebrities were coming and going every five minutes.

The kitchen table was filled with clothing and bedding, so Leah put the plate of stew on the coffee table in front of her uncle.

Uncle Eli picked up his spoon. "Where's the boss?"

Leah grinned. "Aunt Flo's down in her bedroom. Is it true, Uncle Eli, that the population of Gander will double?"

He dipped bread in his stew. "Well, there's thirty-eight planes, most of them with two to three hundred passengers. You do the math." He winked at Leah. "But don't worry, Aunt Flo will have them all organized in no time."

"Why are they all coming here?" Brent asked.

"They're not *all* coming here," Uncle Eli said. "Planes have been landing in St. John's, Deer Lake,

Stephenville — and all across Canada."

"Eli," Aunt Flo said, entering the room. "I didn't hear you come in." She turned on the television. "Millie says President Bush is giving a speech at ten o'clock." She glanced at her watch. "Just a few minutes from now."

Leah lifted her gaze to the television screen. Ground Zero, as the reporters called the gap where the towers once stood, was still smoldering. Firemen and other rescue workers were searching among the rubble for bodies and survivors.

"What a godforsaken mess," Eli said.

"Breaks me heart," Aunt Flo added. "When I think of all them poor people that come in on the planes, I could cry. God only knows what's going through their minds. Must be scared to death. I know I'd be." She settled herself on the sofa, picked up the remote, and turned up the volume. "Kevin said some of them looked shell-shocked when they got off the plane." She looked from Granny to Leah. "We must help the best we can."

"Of course, we'll do whatever it takes," said Granny.

"Millie's taken a family to her basement apartment." Aunt Flo continued. "Wish I had the room."

Not a chance, Leah thought. The house was small and overcrowded already. Aunt Flo had turned her sewing room into a temporary bedroom for Uncle Eli as it was.

When no one answered, Aunt Flo sniffed. "Well, there's other ways we can help, I knows that." She turned her attention back to the television.

"We are awaiting the arrival of President Bush," Wolf Blitzer said from the CNN newsroom. "Any minute now, he will be speaking from the Oval Office."

"Looks like that guy's got coconut stuck to his face." Brent said, eyeing Wolf Blitzer's graying beard.

"For heaven's sake," Aunt Flo interrupted. She put her arm around Brent. "The president is going to talk about the attack."

"President Bush has just now entered the Oval Office," Wolf Blitzer announced. "He's getting ready to address the nation."

The phone rang, and Brent jumped up to answer it.

Cameras moved in so that the president's face filled the screen. "Today, our fellow citizens, our way of life, our very freedom came under attack," he said.

Leah sat with her hands folded in her lap, barely listening. *Dad died when that building he was working on caught fire. Did he jump to his death, like some of the people at the World Trade Center?* It hurt too much to think about. Even now, three years later, she found it hard to talk about.

Leah was so lost in her thoughts, she didn't hear Brent calling from the kitchen. "Leah? You deaf? You're wanted on the phone."

"Phone? At this hour?" Leah got up from the sofa. In the kitchen, the phone dangled on its cord. "Hello?"

"Leah?"

"Mom! Hi." Leah's mom rarely got a chance to call. When she wasn't working, she was studying.

"How's everything?" her mother asked. "You okay?"

"Thousands of passengers landed at the airport this afternoon."

"I know. A number of planes were diverted to Deer Lake and Stephenville as well. As a matter of fact, we treated some of them in the emergency room here."

"Were they sick?"

"Symptoms were mostly stress related. One poor guy thought he was having a heart attack. He was finding it hard to breathe." She paused. "Leah, the reason I'm calling is to tell you I can't make it home this weekend."

Leah clutched the phone. In the background she could hear President Bush. *Today our nation saw evil, the very worst of human nature.* "Do you want me and Brent to take the bus to Corner Brook?" Sometimes, instead of coming home, Mom had Leah and Brent go to her.

"No, honey. I'm gonna be so busy, I won't be able to spend any time with you."

Leah was disappointed. She missed her mom terribly. And since the attack on the United States, she felt like she really needed to be with her mother. "What about the week after?"

Her mom sighed. "I may not be able to see you until the following week."

Leah tried to keep her voice steady. "Well, whenever it's good for you." She wasn't going to let her mom know how upset she was. Things had not been easy for her mother since Dad had died. She'd gone back to school after being out for fifteen years. Leah knew she was making sacrifices to give Brent and her a better future.

"Thanks honey, I knew you'd understand. Give my love to Granny, Aunt Flo, and Uncle Eli. And Leah… could you put Brent back on? I forgot to ask him about his science report."

"Sure, Mom," Leah signed off and went into the living room, but Brent wasn't there. The president was just wrapping up his speech. "None of us will ever forget this day. Yet, we go forward to defend freedom and all that is good and just in the world." Down the hall, Brent's bedroom door was slightly ajar, the room dark. Leah was about to knock when she heard the irregular intake of breath. Brent was crying.

Chapter 13

Rabia lay awake for a long time, staring into the darkness. Beside her, in the double bed, Mama snored softly. She replayed the newscaster's words in her mind. *After the attack on Pearl Harbor, Japanese Americans were rounded up and put in prison.* Would Americans blame Muslims for the attack on the buildings in New York? The attacks were carried out from Afghanistan, after all. To outsiders, it must appear that Islam was a religion of violence. A religion where warriors were eager to kill and die in Allah's name. The more Rabia thought, the harder it was to breathe.

She understood now why the girl at the airport was so hostile. She saw Rabia and her family as enemies. Would people want revenge? Father often said fear causes people to do desperate things. She recalled the women in the bathroom at the airport. *President Bush should go in and drop a bomb on the place.* Rabia realized that it was Afghanistan they were talking about. But had her country not been bombed enough already? The Russians left Kabul in shambles. More than a million Afghans had been killed. Six million more were forced to flee as refugees.

Still, she could understand why the Americans would be fearful. Terrorists had come onto their land and attacked them. It must have been horrible for people who lost family members. Rabia knew what it was like to lose the people she loved. In Kabul, entire families were wiped out. Many of Rabia's classmates had been killed.

Rabia tried to slow her breathing. Her people were *not* responsible for the attacks. Osama bin Laden was *not* one of them. He was a foreigner driven out of his own country. Everyone in Kabul had heard of him. He owned a palace in Kandahar with gold water taps and jeweled doorknobs. He had set up a terrorist organization called Al-Qaeda. Yes, they were Muslims, but they did not practice their faith in the way Rabia and her family practiced theirs. Like the Taliban, Al-Qaeda followed a very fanatical form of religion. They did not follow the teachings of the Qur'an. If they did, they would know that such violence was against Allah's will. They would know it was wrong to kill innocent people. Father said

Al-Qaeda was built on hate and destruction that could only be harmful for Afghanistan.

Rabia pulled her knees to her chest, the pain of loneliness weighing down on her. What would it be like for them in America if they were seen as enemies? Maybe they would be better off going back. But going back to what? She was tired of running from the Taliban, tired of accepting food from relatives who had nothing themselves. Aunt Roxanne and Sima were no better off than slaves, working dawn to dusk in exchange for a room in a shabby basement.

Rabia recalled the day she and Sima watched *Titanic* in the children's playroom. Her cousin had wept for a life she could never have. In Pakistan, she would never have a chance to have an education. She would be trapped in a marriage with a man she did not love.

Rabia managed to take a deep breath. No wonder women in Kabul were drawn to movies like *Titanic*. So many of them had arranged or forced marriages. Secretly, they were hoping someone like Jack would come along and break them out of a world that kept them imprisoned. *I want my life to be better than that*, Rabia told herself. *I deserve a better life*. Father would want her to go to America, she knew.

"No," Rabia whispered into the darkened room. "I will *never* go back."

Chapter 14
September 12

Colin stared at the unfamiliar ceiling. It took a few moments before the memories of yesterday came rushing back. He was in Canada. Gander, Newfoundland, Canada. He looked around the room. Mom lay on her cot, eyes closed, but Colin could tell she was awake. The other families were gone, their blankets and sleeping bags folded neatly on cots and mattresses. Knapsacks, coats, books, and stuffed animals were placed carefully on top. He hadn't even heard them get up.

Colin stayed still, wondering what he should do. He would look for a payphone, he decided. He would try to reach Grant in New York. Grant would know why the planes had been sent here.

No sooner had Colin gotten up from his mattress than he heard a knock at the door. He opened it, and the aroma of frying bacon and freshly brewed coffee wafted into the classroom. A woman holding toothbrushes and towels stood in the hallway. Three kids, a girl and two boys, were standing behind her. For a long moment, Colin stared at them. The girl had dark hair and dark eyes. One of the boys wore a Batman T-shirt, the other a ball hat with Newfie B'y written across the front.

"I hope I didn't wake you," the woman said. She was about Grandma's age with short graying hair. "I'm Flo Goodridge, and this is Leah, Brent, and Jason."

"Hi," he said, "I'm Colin, and…" he pointed to the cot, "that's my mom, Catherine."

The woman walked past Colin into the room. The children followed behind her. "You okay, my dear?" she asked. "You looks right pale, sure."

"A migraine," Catherine said. "Had it since yesterday."

Flo fussed like a mother hen. "Just what you needs along with everything else that's been goin' on." She turned to the children. "Why don't yeh take Colin over to the house so his mom can rest." She looked at Catherine. "If it's okay with you, that is."

Who are *these people?* Colin wondered.

Catherine moaned and rolled over.

"Go get yeh coat, my love," the woman said.

Colin's eyes widened. Mom was forever telling him

never to go with strangers. How could she let him leave with these people? He didn't even know their last name. Well, if he got kidnapped or murdered by Newfie B'y and his gang, it would be all her fault. Picking up his coat, he followed the trio to the door.

"Make sure he gets something to eat," Flo called after them.

As they walked to the front door, Colin saw that tables had been set up and men and women in aprons were serving breakfast to the stranded passengers. As he was leaving the building, a couple of people arrived with trays of food.

"We lives just over there," one of the boys said when they were outside. He pointed vaguely.

They walked down tree-lined streets, the trees just starting to give up their color. The houses were well kept with neatly trimmed lawns. Within fifteen minutes, they came to a small white bungalow where flowers bloomed in flowerbeds on the lawn.

"That you, Flo?" a voice called as they opened the front door.

"No, Granny," Leah said. "Aunt Flo's at the school, helping the plane people."

Colin followed the others into a large kitchen. Leah opened the fridge. "What would you like to eat?" she asked Colin. "There's baked beans I can heat up. Or, if you like, I can make some toast."

Colin wasn't hungry, but his mouth felt dry. "Can I please just have something to drink?"

Leah reached into the fridge and took out three sodas. She handed one to Colin, and offered the other two cans to Batman and Newfie B'y.

Mom would have a fit if she knew I was drinking soda before breakfast, he thought. *But then again, maybe not. She doesn't even seem to care where I am, let alone what I'm having for breakfast.*

They moved into the living room. Colin was about to sit down when he caught sight of a small TV on a stand. The sound was muted, but he recognized the twin towers of the World Trade Center on the screen. Maybe if he could listen to the news, he might find out what was happening back home. He watched with interest as the New York skyline filled the small screen. An airplane seemed to come out of nowhere, gliding across the clear sky. But why was it flying so close to the World Trade Center? Had it veered off course? Then, without warning, the plane crashed soundlessly into one of the towers. A great ball of fire and smoke rose into the sky. Colin stared in horror as panic-stricken people on the ground scrambled away from the tower. What he'd heard was true then! The United States *was* under attack. Hijackers *were* flying planes into buildings. His apartment was near the twin towers. It would probably be destroyed by the time they got home. *If* they got home.

Colin opened his mouth, but was unable to speak. But he must have made some sound because Granny came bustling down the hallway. "What's wrong?"

"Buddy from the plane," Newfie B'y said. "He's upset."

Colin pointed to the television, his whole body trembling as the north tower crumbled like a sand castle. "It's true," he said, finding his voice. "It's all true!" His knees buckled.

"Oh, you poor youngster." Granny's bony arms encircled his shoulders. "Didn't nobody tell yeh what happened?" She led him to a nearby chair and motioned him to sit.

Colin listened in horror as she told him about the terrorist attack. "Some hooligans flew a plane into the towers," Granny explained. "Happened yesterday. But don't worry, my son. Everything's under control now."

Colin sank down in the nearest chair. The pain in his throat so terrible he could hardly breathe. Who would do such a horrible thing? He was stranded in a strange country. New York seemed so terribly far away.

Chapter 15
September 13

Rabia picked up a tray from the table and began gathering plates and cups. For the past couple of hours she had been helping Millie serve lunch to passengers sheltered at a school. She liked the work; it helped take her mind off all the bad things that had happened. A steady stream of volunteers arrived regularly with home cooking and drinks. There were tables filled with platters of food and dessert. Rabia didn't have much of an appetite, but this act of kindness by strangers somehow lessened her fear.

She had heard on television this morning that a number of mosques in the United States had been threatened. In some places, Muslim businesses had been vandalized. There was even talk that the president would go to war against Afghanistan. Yousef once told her that the United States was the most powerful country in the world. Like the Soviets, they could destroy the whole world with one press of a button. The tightness in Rabia's throat made it hard to breathe. She had family in Afghanistan — people she loved and cared about. Father was still there. She could not bear it if more destruction came to her country. *It is all because of you, Osama bin Laden,* she thought, feeling a wave of resentment. *Do you realize what you have done to us?*

"Are you going on the trip this afternoon?" Millie asked, interrupting her thoughts.

"Trip?"

"Yes, my dear. Some fishermen down in Salvage volunteered to take the passengers out in their boats."

"On the ocean?" Rabia asked. Father had told her about the ocean, and how it smelled of salt. The ocean was so large, he said, that sometimes all one could see was water and sky. She bet Karim would love to go on a trip like that. But how much would it cost? What little money they had was only to be used for emergencies.

"It's free," Millie said as if reading her thoughts.

"How can we get there?"

"A bus is coming by this afternoon to pick up the passengers."

Rabia was thoughtful.

"Oh, my dear, you should go," Millie said. "Get to see whales, sure. Someone spotted an iceberg out there this morning. Not something you'd expect to see this late in the season. Won't see much of that stuff once you gets to California."

Before Rabia had a chance to respond, the woman and boy who had got on the plane in England came into the room. Rabia watched as they took a seat at one of the tables. The boy opened his book and stared at the page. His forehead furrowed in concentration.

Millie walked over to their table. "Can I get you something?"

"May I have some coffee, please?" the woman asked.

"I will get it," Rabia offered, eager to help.

Millie turned to the boy. "How about you, my love? Milk? Juice?"

"Orange juice, please," he said without looking up from his game.

Rabia poured the coffee and brought it back to the table. "Hello," she said shyly, not sure if they remembered her.

The woman smiled at her. "Thank you. The coffee smells wonderful."

The boy gave Rabia an icy stare and went back to his book. All the friendliness he had shown her on the airplane was gone.

Millie brought a juice pack over and put it in front of Colin. "Where are you from?" she asked.

"New York City," the woman replied. "I'm Catherine Erickson and this is my son, Colin."

"My," Millie said. "I'm meeting people from all over the world." She put a hand on Rabia's shoulder. "Sure, Rabia came all the way from Afghanistan."

Colin looked up from his book. "Afghanistan. Isn't that the same place Osama bin Laden is hiding?"

Rabia did not miss the hostility in his voice. She was so dumbfounded by his remark that for a moment, she didn't respond. Then she folded her arms across her chest, dark eyes flashing. "Yes," she said. "Same place."

Colin fixed her with an accusing glare.

Catherine Erickson smiled apologetically at Rabia. "I hope you enjoy your visit."

"I go to America to live."

"To live!" Colin scoffed. "After what your people did? Good luck."

"My people...they do nothing."

The boy was about to say something else, but his mother put a hand on his arm. "Colin..." she warned.

"Rabia, my love," Millie said. "Maybe you should run home if you're going on that trip this afternoon. Can you find your way back to the house? I'll call Jason if you like."

"No. It is okay." Rabia took off her apron. "I will walk."

So, this is how it is going to be, she thought as she walked back to Millie's house. Who did that boy think he was? She could hear Father's voice in her head. *People act unreasonably out of fear, Rabia. Maybe so*, she thought, struggling to contain her anger. *But it is hard to feel sympathy for this ill-mannered boy.*

When she reached the driveway, Jason and Karim were just leaving the house. Although her brother was shy with strangers, he seemed to have formed a special bond with Jason.

"Hi Rabia," Jason called. "We're going over to Aunt Flo's. Want to come along?"

"How is Mama?" Rabia asked. Mama wasn't feeling well when Rabia left the house that morning.

"She's sleeping," Jason told her.

"Then I will come," Rabia said, falling into step beside him.

"Are you okay?" Jason asked.

"Fine," she answered. There was no way she was going to admit that some silly American boy had upset her.

Chapter 16

Catherine frowned at Colin over the rim of her coffee cup. "How could you be so rude to that poor girl? None of this is her fault."

Colin shrugged. After seeing the towers plummet to the ground yesterday, it was as if something cold and hard had curled around his heart. And for some reason the girl really bothered him. Maybe it was the stubborn way her small chin tilted in defiance. More and more Muslims were coming to the United States all the time. "How do we know she's not a terrorist?" he said.

"Colin, for heaven's sake! Listen to yourself. You can't go making a judgment every time you see someone in a headscarf."

"I heard the president on television in the teacher's

lounge yesterday morning," he told her. "He says he'll bring in Osama bin Laden, dead or alive."

Catherine cocked an eyebrow. "Charming."

Colin took a sip from his juice pack. For a long time, they sat in silence. He couldn't get the image of planes flying into the towers out of his head. From time to time, a quiet sadness crept through him like a wisp of smoke. The looming towers of the World Trade Center were always the first things he saw when he got up each morning. In second grade, his teacher had taken them there on a field trip. He learned that each tower had one hundred and ten floors. Now they were reduced to a huge heap of ash and rubble. Ground Zero.

Studying his face, Catherine reached across the table and covered his hand briefly. "We'll get through this," she said.

Colin nodded. At least his family was safe. Many of the stranded passengers had family members they hadn't been able to reach.

Earlier this morning his mother had walked to Newtel, the Newfoundland telephone company. Tables with cell phones had been set up on the sidewalk in front of their offices so passengers could make free long-distance calls to family and friends. Mom called London, and Grandma informed her that Dad had phoned from Africa after hearing about the attack. She had also called a number of her friends and co-workers to make sure they were okay.

Colin used the free service to call his friend Grant. He left a message saying he was in Canada, that he would call again soon, and to hug Jake for him. What he should have done, he realized now, was to leave the Goodridge's phone number.

"Well, look who's here," Catherine said, jolting Colin out of his thoughts. "Leah."

Colin looked toward the door. Leah waved as she approached them. She was wearing jeans and a pink hooded sweater, her dark hair pulled back into a ponytail.

"Leah, good to see you, dear," Catherine said. "Is your Aunt Flo volunteering here again today?"

"Aunt Flo had to go back to work. But, she's invited you and Colin to a barbeque this evening."

"A barbeque! Sounds wonderful. What time is she expecting us?"

"She said before seven." Leah turned to Colin. "I was wondering if you want to hang out at our house today."

Colin looked at his mom.

"Go ahead," she said. "I'm going to enjoy a second cup of coffee."

Colin picked up his empty juice pack and dropped it in the garbage. He'd been to Leah's house twice already, and Granny and Aunt Flo had welcomed him like family. *What would it be like to live in Gander?* he wondered. *Neighbors drop in on each other unannounced and no one seems to mind at all.*

On the way to her house, Leah told Colin about a phone call from her mother who was away in Corner Brook, training to be a nurse. "A man was brought to the hospital this morning," Leah said. "He was found in a ditch. Someone robbed him and left him there. He's still unconscious, so they don't even know who he is."

"That's a shame," Colin said politely, but wondered why Leah was telling him this. People got mugged all the time in New York.

"The police put out a statement asking if anyone had information about the man," Leah continued. "Trouble is, he can't be properly identified because his face was beaten so badly. But," she added, "he has a scar on his leg."

"Lots of people have scars," Colin said, on reaching the house. "My dad has a scar on *his* leg." He shrugged. "I suppose though, it will be helpful in identifying him."

When Colin walked into the kitchen, he stopped abruptly. Brent, Jason, and another boy sat around the table eating. And who should be with them but the girl from Afghanistan — the girl who had been at the shelter less than an hour ago.

"What's *she* doing here?" Colin whispered.

Leah introduced everyone. Rabia seemed as surprised to see Colin as he was to see her.

"We're having some of Granny's bakeapples," Jason said.

Granny took a couple of bowls down from the cupboard. "You're just in time to have some yourself," she told Colin.

"I should have warned you," Leah whispered. "Granny makes everyone try her bakeapples."

"Bakeapples?"

"Berries," Leah explained. She pulled out a chair for Colin to sit down. "They taste good with cream and sugar." She took a seat across from him at the table.

Colin shook his head. What odd people they were. In the short time he'd been in Newfoundland, he'd eaten so many strange foods. Last evening someone had brought moose burgers to the shelter.

Granny put a bowl in front of him and spooned the orange berries out of a bottle. She opened a can of cream and put it in a dish on the table. "Any word about when the planes are leaving?"

"None so far." Colin watched Leah sprinkle sugar on her bakeapples and add a dab of cream. He followed suit, aware of the girl across the table, her dark eyes watching him. He lifted a spoonful of berries to his mouth. They tasted like peaches, but more tangy.

"I heard there might be terrorists on the plane," Jason said.

"That's why they wouldn't allow the planes into the States," Colin said grimly. He looked pointedly at Rabia and Karim. "They could be among us, just waiting to kill us."

"Oh, my!" said Granny.

"They hate us," Colin said.

Granny studied him with interest. "Why is that, my love?"

"Our president says it's because we have so much freedom." Colin put down his spoon. "President Bush is going to hunt down Osama bin Laden — smoke him out of his cave."

Granny's lips twitched. "Tough words."

Jason pushed back his chair. "We should be going," he told the others, "if we're going on that trip this afternoon." He carried the bowls to the sink. "Thanks for the bakeapples, Granny."

"You're more than welcome, my love. Have fun in Salvage."

Jason headed for the door, Rabia and Karim following.

"That poor girl had her foot blown off in a landmine," Granny said when the door closed behind them.

A landmine? Colin paled slightly. He didn't like her, but still…

"Ah, 'tis a wicked world we lives in." Granny met Colin's gaze. "How's your poor mother?"

"She's been fine since her headache went away," he told her. "She called Grandma in London this morning. Grandma told her that my dad called from Kenya."

"Your dad's not in New York?"

"No," Colin said, wishing he could take back his words. He hated having to explain why his parents weren't together. "Dad's in Kenya. His work takes him all over the world."

Granny didn't see anything strange about that at all. She said that three of her grandsons had to leave their families to go out to Alberta to look for work. Leah's dad had worked in construction before he got killed. One year, he went to a place called Fort McMurray. Left in July, and didn't get home until Christmas.

Granny smiled. "Got any other relations in New York?"

"No, but my friends are there. I've been trying to reach my friend Grant to make sure he and his family are okay." He looked from Granny to Leah. "Would it be okay if I left your telephone number on Grant's answering machine? That way, he could call and leave a message."

106

"Go ahead, my love. Call from here." Granny nodded toward the telephone on the kitchen wall.

"Thank you," Colin said, tipping his bowl to get the last of the berries. He took the dish to the sink, went to the phone, and dialed Grant's number from memory. The phone rang three times before it was picked up. The Taylors hardly ever answered their phone, so Colin was surprised to hear Grant's voice.

"Grant? It's me, Colin."

"Colin! I got your message. You're in Canada?"

"Our plane was diverted," he explained. "How are things?"

"Very sad since Nelson and David came crashing down," Grant said grimly. "Nothing but a pile of rubble now."

Colin swallowed over a lump in his throat. "Must have been hard, seeing it all."

"I was in school when it happened. We watched from the window." Colin heard a catch in Grant's voice. "It...it was horrible. Ben Dillard's dad was killed."

"Oh, that's *terrible*." Ben was a boy in their class. "And how are you, Grant? Is Jake okay?"

"We're doing okay. Jake too, but I think he misses you. Does your dad know where you are?"

"Dad called Grandma in London right after he heard about the attack."

"Called from New York?"

"Dad's in Kenya," Colin said. Grant knew that.

"Your dad was in New York on September 11," Grant said. "He called our house shortly before the planes hit the towers."

Colin sucked in his breath. "Are you sure?"

"I took the call. He wanted to know your flight number."

Colin gripped the receiver, his heart racing. "Dad was calling from New York?"

"Said he was in Lower Manhattan. Mom had the flight information, but she was in the shower. Your dad was on his way to his friend Ed's office so he said he'd call back for the flight number when he got there." There was a slight pause. "He never called back."

Colin dropped into the nearest chair. Ed Nestor was a lawyer. His office was in the twin towers of the World Trade Center. Dad often went to him for advice concerning his work. If he had gone there just before the attack.... A chill went up Colin's spine. *But Mom told me that Dad had called Grandma from Kenya. Mom lied. Why? Was it to protect me from the truth?* It felt as if all the air had been sucked out of the room.

Dad was missing.

Chapter 17

Rabia was already on the bus when it pulled up in front of the academy. Eli had stopped for them after he picked up Leah and Brent. Rabia wore one of Millie's jackets, and Karim had on a thick woolen sweater that belonged to Jason. Millie had warned them it would get chilly on the ocean.

Through the window, Rabia saw Colin waiting in line with the other people. She had been hoping he wouldn't come on the trip. Colin didn't like her, that much was clear. Did he think she enjoyed having to flee her country because of the Taliban? *I will not let him ruin my day,* she decided, as she watched him climb aboard.

"Colin," Leah called, patting the seat beside her. "Glad you made it."

He moved down the aisle without a glance at Rabia. Still, she could not help noticing the worried look on his face. Clearly, he was troubled. Something must have happened since she saw him at Leah's house.

Eli pulled out of the parking lot, and Rabia turned her face to the window. The bus moved down the main street, past houses and brick buildings with large glass windows. It stopped at places called the Lions Club, the Knights of Columbus, and other shelters that housed stranded passengers. It was not long before the bus was full.

It was close to two-thirty by the time they rolled into Salvage. Rabia stared in awe at the ocean before her. Never had she seen so much water. It seemed to go on forever. It was the color of pewter, not the deep green she had so often seen in pictures. Still, it was every bit as fascinating.

The village had no more than a couple of dozen houses scattered about on rocky hills and cliffs. A grave-yard with headstones and wooden crosses sloped toward the sea.

"Oohs" and "ahhs" came from the delighted passengers as the bus bounced down a winding narrow path.

Rabia stared out the window at the fishing boats and wharves cluttered with lobster pots, nets, and crates.

"Get a load of that," she heard Colin say. It was

another of those strange expressions Canadians and Americans used.

"A typical little fishing village," said one of the passengers. "Looks like something you'd see on a postcard."

Rabia's heart pounded with excitement as she took in the colorful boats tied up at the wharves. Before long, she would be cruising on the ocean.

"Can we get off to take pictures?" someone asked.

"Five minutes," Eli told them, glancing at his watch. "We shouldn't keep the fishermen waiting."

Rabia got off the bus with the others while Karim stayed with Jason. Seagulls flapped over wharves and fish stages, squawking loudly. Rabia could taste the salt in the moist air just as Father had described it. Mama would have liked this place, she knew. Too bad she wasn't feeling well. Rabia glanced at the flat, gray rocks along the beach. Perfect building blocks. Maybe when they got to California she would find rocks like that for Karim. Maybe he would take an interest in building things again.

They got back on the bus, and Eli drove to the wharf where the boats were waiting. Fishermen organized the passengers into groups of twelve. A faint odor of tar and fish filled Rabia's nostrils as she boarded the *Molly Rose*, a boat owned by an old fisherman named Moses. The engine thudded, and soon she was moving out to sea, a cold wind on her face, flattening her jacket against her chest. Cold water sprayed her face and the sting of salt made her eyes water. The ocean was everything Rabia had imagined and more. She was mesmerized by the sheer size of it. Miles and miles of gray as far as she could see. She felt her spirits rising as a feeling of calm settled over her. For a little while she was able to forget everything bad that had happened.

Not far out, some of the passengers began to point excitedly. "I see an iceberg," someone shouted.

Rabia shaded her eyes with her hands to get a better look at the towering mountain of white in the distance.

"Now that's a rarity if I ever seen one," Eli said. He stopped the engine and let the boat drift toward the iceberg. "Don't think I ever seen one of those this late in the season."

Eager passengers held up cameras. Rabia had never seen anything so sparkling white. It radiated an icy coldness that she felt in her nostrils and at the back of her throat. It was an iceberg such as this that had destroyed the great *Titanic*.

As they drew closer, Rabia noticed it was an odd shape. The icebergs she had seen in pictures were mostly shaped like triangles with pointed tops. This one was shaped like an upside down U, big enough for the boat to drive through. Father once told her that seven eighths of an iceberg is underwater.

"Can we get closer?" someone asked.

"We're close enough," Eli said. "Sometimes icebergs will roll and can upset a boat. Makes it dangerous for people who harvest them." He looked at the bewildered passengers. "In Newfoundland, icebergs are harvested to make vodka," he explained. "Sometimes they're sold as gourmet ice cubes."

"How do they harvest them?" A man asked.

"Ice wranglers," Eli replied. "They lasso the bergs, tows them to shore, and cuts them up with chainsaws." He smiled. "They're gonna start producing bottled water to sell to the United States. Some of you could be drinking that iceberg sometime soon."

"Cool," a woman said. Another one of those strange expressions Rabia would have to try out when she got to California.

Rabia squeezed Karim's hand. How she wished Father could share this moment with them. In America he had picked up an expression: *Just the tip of the iceberg*. He used the phrase when he described the corrupt warlords in Afghanistan. What would Father say about the attack on the United States? Was that also just the tip of the iceberg?

• • •

"Wow! What an outing," Colin said to Leah as the bus rolled into town.

"Yeah," Leah agreed. "And that iceberg was awesome."

Colin nodded, absently. He'd enjoyed the trip, in spite of the concern for Dad that hovered like a dark cloud at the back of his mind.

"Are you okay?" Leah asked. "You seem…I don't know…someplace else."

Colin sighed. "Remember the phone call I made from your house this afternoon?"

"Yeah."

"Well, turns out Dad may have been at the World Trade Center during the attack."

"But you said he was in Kenya," Leah said, studying the grave look on Colin's face.

"He arrived in New York on the morning of September 11th. He called my friend Grant shortly before the towers fell to get our flight information." Colin's voice trembled. "He said he was on his way to the World Trade Center to see his lawyer."

"Oh, Colin! No wonder you're worried." Leah peered at him with concern. "Does your mom know?"

"Mom lied to me," Colin said, feeling betrayed. "Dad called Grandma from New York, not Kenya, as my mom said."

"Why would she say that?"

Colin met Leah's gaze. "To protect me from the truth, I imagine. She's always trying to protect me in some way or another. She thinks it's for my own good."

"My mother is like that," Leah sympathized. "My aunt too."

"Well, I'm going to let Mom know how I feel," Colin said with determination. "If Dad's missing, I have a right to know."

Leah put her hand on his arm. "Best to pretend you don't know anything."

Colin looked puzzled. "Why?"

"You'll find out more that way," Leah said. "Trust me, I know. Mom and Aunt Flo want what's best for me, but sometimes they treat me like a little kid. I had to find out things about my dad's death from kids who'd heard it from *their* parents."

Leah had a point, Colin had to admit.

"Not that I believe anything bad happened to your father," she hurried on. "Granny says things are never as bad as we imagine them."

The bus had pulled up in front of the academy, and people were getting off.

Colin stood up. "Thanks for today, Leah. I guess I'll see you at the barbeque."

"Okay, Colin."

When Colin walked into the classroom, his mother was sitting on her cot, talking on her cell phone. She must have had the code changed, he realized. He was about to call out a greeting when he heard her say "I don't see any reason to worry Colin."

Colin frowned. It was just as he thought.

As if sensing someone behind her, she turned around. "I should go, Mother. Colin is back from his trip. Yes, I'll tell him." She signed off, flipped the phone shut and put it in her purse.

"Hi, Colin," she said. "I didn't hear you come in."

Obviously not, he thought.

"I was talking to Grandma. She sends her love."

"Cool," Colin said, his voice casual. *Leah's right. Best to pretend I don't know what's going on.*

He reached for the book Grandma had given him. He'd already read it twice, but every now and then, he liked to read his favorite parts. He especially liked Odysseus's encounter with the Sirens — singing sea nymphs whose beautiful voices lured sailors to their islands. But the chapter he enjoyed most was the one where Odysseus returned home disguised as an old man. Even his wife didn't recognize him.

Colin flipped through the pages, unable to

concentrate. *Where was Dad? When was Mom going to admit he was missing? How long did Mom she think she could go on fooling him?*

Chapter 18

Karim saw the ambulance first. They had just said good-bye to Leah and Brent and had turned onto their street when Karim pulled on Rabia's arm. She followed his gaze to the driveway where a long white vehicle was parked.

"An ambulance," Jason said, sounding worried.

Rabia stopped in her tracks, a cold fear settling over her. Had something happened to Mama? Her heart raced as she tried to swallow back her panic. She watched, frozen, as two men slid a collapsed gurney through the rear doors. One of them climbed into the back. The other closed the doors and got into the driver's seat. The siren wailed with an urgency that set Rabia's heart pounding. She watched in shocked silence as the ambulance sped out of the driveway, red lights flashing.

Grabbing Karim's hand, she ran toward the house

with Jason close behind. "What happened?" he called out to his mother, who was standing in the doorway.

Millie walked down the driveway to meet them. She put her hand on Rabia's shoulder. "It's your mother, my love," she said. "I went downstairs to bring her some food. She was having trouble breathing, so I called 911."

Rabia's knees felt as if they would give way. She wanted to cry, but it felt as if a ball of wool had been stuffed down her throat. *This cannot be happening,* she told herself. She was shaking uncontrollably.

"Come inside." Millie took her arm and led her into the house. Karim followed behind them, his face somber.

Rabia crumpled into a chair near the fireplace. "Mama...will she be okay?" She asked in a quiet voice.

Millie poured a cup of tea from the pot on the stove and handed it to her. "I'm sure they will do everything they can to help her, my love."

"Can I go to her?" Rabia fought to keep her voice steady. She had to see her; she couldn't let Mama be in a strange hospital alone.

"Of course." Millie picked up the phone. "I'm trying to get a hold of Kevin. The van is in the garage. God knows how long it will be before 'tis ready."

"What is wrong with Mama?" Rabia asked.

"Does she have a bad heart?"

Rabia shook her head. But what did she know?

Mama never went to visit a doctor. In Kabul, the Taliban forbade women to go to male doctors, and female doctors were not allowed to practice.

"The paramedics asked me all kinds of questions," Millie said. "Was she on any medications. If she had any food or drug allergies. I couldn't tell them a thing. I don't even know her age."

"She take no medicine. She is forty-four years."

"Only forty-four. Oh, my dear." Millie got up off the sofa. "I'll call the hospital, give them the information, and ask them to get in touch with me as soon as they know something. I imagine they'll take her to Western Memorial in Corner Brook. Hospital here in town is filled up, they tells me."

"I should not have left her," Rabia said, feeling a sharp sting of guilt. Mama had told her she was not feeling well. She should have stayed home and taken care of her instead of going on the trip.

"No, my love, it wasn't your fault," Millie assured her. "Just be thankful she's where she can get help." She put a comforting hand on Rabia's arm. "Soon as the van is fixed, we'll take you to your mother."

A wave of weariness shot through Rabia. She had been so sure that going to America was best for all of them. Now clouds of doubt filled her mind. Everything was going so terribly wrong.

Chapter 19

It was nearly six-thirty by the time Colin and his mother pulled into Aunt Flo's driveway in a taxi. They had stopped at the bakery and picked up a cheesecake. A number of people had already arrived for the barbeque and were sitting on lawn chairs around a small bonfire. Brent and some of his friends were running around the yard with water pistols.

"My dear, you didn't have to take a taxi," Aunt Flo said. "Sure, Eli could have picked you up."

"I made a trip to the market," Catherine said, handing Aunt Flo the white box.

"Oh, my dear, no need for that. But how thoughtful." She put the box on a side table that held squares and cookies.

"Hi, Colin," Leah said, coming into the kitchen. "Hi, Mrs. Erickson."

"Please call me Catherine." She smiled at Leah. "Colin told me he had a wonderful time this afternoon. I'm sorry I missed it."

"Everyone enjoyed the trip," Leah said.

"Interesting to learn that people actually harvest icebergs. I read somewhere that seventy percent of the world's fresh water is locked up in icecaps."

"Since the fishery collapsed, people are looking for other ways to make a living," Aunt Flo said. She picked up a plate of steaks from the counter. "Everyone's outside. Why don't you come meet them?"

Catherine nodded. "I'm looking forward to it."

"Can I borrow your cell phone, Mom?" Colin asked.

She took the phone from her purse, and handed it to Colin. "It might still be difficult getting through to New York," she said, as she followed Aunt Flo outside.

Colin turned to Leah. "How's it going?"

"I just got off the phone with my mother. Uncle Eli is driving to Port-aux-Basques late tonight, and I was hoping to ride with him as far as Corner Brook. Mom said it was out of the question. She's too busy with her work and her studies." Leah folded her arms across her chest. "It's not like I expect her to stay home and babysit me. I'm okay in the apartment alone while she's at work."

"You must be really disappointed."

Leah nodded.

Colin flipped open the cell. "I have to call my dad's friend."

"If you need privacy, you can use my room," Leah told him.

"No, it's okay." Colin punched in Ed Nestor's home number. It was easy to remember: 222-NEST. The phone rang three times before it was picked up.

"Mr. Nestor?" Colin was relieved to hear Ed's voice. "It's Colin Erickson speaking. Are you okay?"

"Oh, Colin. Yes, I was just arriving at work when the first plane hit the tower. All of the staff was able to get out. Thank God."

"I'm glad you're okay."

"Thanks Colin. What about you? Are you still in Newfoundland?"

"How did you know I was here?"

"Your father told me."

"Dad?" Colin held his breath.

"When were you talking to Dad?"

"Tuesday morning, just after his flight got in. He called my cell."

"September 11th? Dad talked to you on September 11th?" Colin asked, his words tumbling out. "What time?"

"Must have been around ten o'clock."

Colin realized he had been holding his breath. He let it out. *Ten o'clock. After the towers fell.*

"Did he arrive in Gander okay?"

"Arrive?"

"He called to tell me he was on his way to find you and your mother. He had made some inquiries and learned where you were."

"Dad's coming here?"

"Should have been there by now," Ed told him. "He was planning to drive to Bar Harbor on Tuesday morning to take the ferry to Yarmouth. He should have been in North Sydney late Wednesday morning or early afternoon." He paused. "Didn't your mother tell you?"

"No," Colin croaked. "And Dad didn't show."

"Maybe he changed his mind about going," Ed said, clearly confused. "Or maybe he's just late getting there."

"Yes," Colin said. "That's probably the case. Ed, if you hear from Dad, please tell him Mom and I are okay."

"Sure thing, Colin. You take care, now."

"Is everything all right?" Leah asked as Colin folded the phone. "You look shaken."

"Dad didn't go to the World Trade Center after all."

Leah peered at him. "Well, that's good news, isn't it?"

"Yes," Colin agreed. "But I still don't know where he is. Ed says he was on his way here."

"Here…? You mean Newfoundland?"

Colin nodded. "According to Ed."

"Does your mother know?"

"I guess so."

Aunt Flo poked her head around the door. "Leah, I need you to go to the Co-op to pick up some more soft drinks."

Leah glanced at Colin.

"I could use the walk," he said.

No sooner had they left the house than a car pulled over. "Need a ride?" the driver shouted. By now, Colin was used to strangers offering rides. Whenever he and his mother were out walking, someone always stopped to ask if they needed a ride. Everyone wanted to make sure the "plane people" were taken care of.

"No thanks, Shirley," Leah called. "We're enjoying the walk."

For a while, they continued in silence.

"Are you going to tell your mother about what you know?" Leah broke the silence.

Colin shrugged. "I don't know. She must have known Dad's plans."

Leah nodded. "I guess…."

Colin's mind raced with unanswered questions. *Did Mom tell Dad not to come? Maybe after the nasty fight they'd had back in the summer, she wanted nothing more to do with him. Of course, it was possible he had changed his plans. Or...* Colin did not want to consider the possibility that something might have happened to his father. The whole thing was worrisome.

The store was crowded with long lines of people waiting at the checkouts. Leah went to find the soft drinks. Colin headed for the magazine rack. When he met Leah back at the checkout, he had picked up a couple of crossword puzzle magazines and a newspaper.

They were going through the checkout when Colin noticed a man a couple of lanes over. There was something familiar about him, he thought, taking in his trendy, red-tinted glasses. Blond highlights were visible in his stylishly cut hair. "I know that man from somewhere," he told Leah. "Can't remember where." He watched as the cashier rang in the man's purchase: a couple of books, peppermints, some pens, and a notepad. "Clemens Briels!" Colin said aloud.

"Huh?"

"That man heading for the door. That's Clemens Briels, the famous Dutch artist."

"Wow! You never know who might be stranded here." Leah paid the cashier and picked up her bag.

"Wait until Grandma hears," Colin said. "Briels is one of her favorite artists."

Before Leah could respond, Millie Keating

126

approached them. "Hello, Leah, my dear," she greeted. "Out gettin' a few things, I see." She nodded at Colin.

"Hi, Millie. I thought you'd be at the barbeque."

"Don't much feel like a party now. My houseguest had a heart attack. She's in the hospital."

"Rabia's mother?"

Millie nodded. "We're leaving early in the morning to take Rabia and Karim to see her. Would've left this evening, but Kevin's van is in the garage. The part he needed didn't come until this afternoon, but the mechanic is making it a priority. Says he'll work on it all night if he has to."

"How is Rabia's mother?" Leah asked.

Millie shrugged. "I called the hospital. They said she's resting comfortably. Poor Rabia is beside herself with worry."

Leah frowned. "How awful."

"Yes," Millie agreed. "Heaven alone knows what them poor youngsters have been through." She lowered her voice. "I thought the little fellar was a deaf mute like poor old Angus Doyle down in Gambo. But, God love him, Rabia told Jason he stopped talking after he'd seen his older brother get killed." She shook her head. "Musta shook him up pretty bad."

"Where will they stay in Corner Brook?" Leah asked.

"The hospital has a hostel for people visiting relatives."

"Rabia must be worried sick," Leah said.

"Seems to me she's the one in charge," Millie said. "I thought it was because she spoke English so well. But..." She shrugged. "I don't know...seems like everything falls on her shoulders." She shook her head, sadly. "I'm glad they have a chance to go live in the States."

Colin was quiet on the walk home. He hadn't realized life had been so difficult for Rabia. Having her brother die must have been terrible. And now her mother was sick. A heart attack was serious. Grandpa had died from a heart attack. What would happen to Karim and Rabia if their mother died? He couldn't imagine being alone in a strange country without at least one of his parents.

Chapter 20

Millie had insisted that Rabia and Karim move upstairs with the family. "I don't want you and your brother staying alone," she told Rabia.

Now Rabia was curled into a tight ball in the middle of the large bed. All she could think about was Mama, alone in a strange hospital not having the language to communicate with anyone. She would get to see Mama tomorrow; Kevin and Millie had promised her that. Still, Rabia felt more alone and more uncertain than she had in her life.

What would they do if Mama did not recover? A host of possibilities passed through her mind, none of them good. No one in America would want to be burdened with two orphans. They would be put on a plane and sent back to Afghanistan. Rabia swallowed to ease the tightness in her throat. *You must not think such hope-less thoughts,* she chided herself. *Mama is going to recover. Soon we will all be on a plane to America.*

Father often told her that when life got rough she should think of something she could be grateful for. *I have a lot of things to be thankful for,* Rabia reminded herself. Kevin and Millie had shown them so much kindness. Tomorrow they were going to take her to her mother at the hospital. Kevin was taking time off work so he could drive her.

Poor Mama. She had not been well for some time now. Bit by bit, her world had fallen apart until her spirits were as shattered as the Buddhas in the Bamiyan Valley.

Through the open bedroom window, Rabia could hear talking and laughter. Jason and his friends were having a sleepover in the backyard. How simple Jason's life was. Never having to worry where his next meal was coming from. He went to school and had plans to go to university. Life had never been so easy for Karim and Rabia.

One by one, Rabia had lost the people she loved: Father, Yousef, Amir. She could not bear to lose Mama too. *At least Amir is safe in Iran,* she told herself. *And Father* — she could only hope her father was still alive. The memory of his arrest still lingered at the dark corners of her mind. Most of the time, she could keep it at bay, but now, images played in her head like a home movie on fast forward. She squeezed her eyes shut, trying to block out the horror if it:

Early February. The streets and rooftops of Kabul are blanketed with freshly fallen snow. Father has cancelled his poetry workshop. He has a feeling something bad is about to happen. Father has a keen sense about such things.

Yousef and Amir are both at their jobs. Karim is running through the house, arms outstretched, making noises like an airplane. Mama is staring out the window at the street. When the Taliban took control, they ordered all windows to be boarded up or painted black. Mama had insisted they keep one window clear. "I will go crazy without sunlight," she complained. Father allowed her to have her window even though they could be severely punished for such an offense. Around mid-afternoon, Mama announces that the Taliban are coming toward the house.

Father scrambles to place a board over the window. He grabs a couple of his poetry books from the table and frantically pulls up the floorboard. He has just put the board in place when two Talibs burst through the door, eyes wild. Mama, Karim, and Rabia have retreated to the far corner of the room.

"Can I help you?" Father asks, his voice calm.

One of the Talibs, the bigger of the two, does all the

131

talking. "*Your beard is not long enough,*" *he says.*

Father wraps his fist around his beard. About half an inch of fuzz shows at the bottom. That is the Taliban rule regarding beards. Mama and Rabia give a collective sigh of relief, although they know the Talibs are not there because of Father's beard. Most likely they have found out about the poetry workshops. In Kabul, neighbors often spy on one another. Someone must have reported them.

"*You have spent time in America,*" *the Talib says.*

Father nods. "*I went to school in Boston.*"

"*You have spent time with the enemy.*"

"*I wanted only to get an education.*"

"*Don't argue.*" *The Talib hits him in the stomach with the butt of his rifle. Father bends over in pain. Rabia puts her hand over her mouth to keep from crying out. Karim's eyes are wide with fright. Mama looks just as scared.*

"*Western morals have corrupted you,*" *the Talib continues.*

"*I am a good Muslim,*" *Father says.* "*I pray five times a day. I go to mosque. I am saving to take my family to the holy land of Mecca.*"

"*Shut up!*" *The Talib roars. He hits Father again, this time on the head. Blood spurts from the wound.*

Rabia rushes forward, fists clenched. She wants to kick the Talib, beat him with her fists. But Father's eyes plead with her. It is clear he does not want her to get hurt. "*Soldier on," he mouths. It is something he says to her whenever things get rough.*

She watches in horror as Father is dragged from the house. Please do not let them harm him, she prays silently. Even though, she knows she can get into serious trouble, Rabia removes the board covering the window. She watches as the Talibs drag Father down the street. Bright red blood flows from the wound on his head, dripping onto the white snow.

● ● ●

Rabia wiped away her tears with the back of her hand. That day was the last time she had seen Father. She had no idea where he was, or if she would ever see him again. But she had to take care of things. She must encourage Mama to get well. Make sure Karim is safe. For Father's sake, she would soldier on.

Chapter 21

Colin took the newspaper from the grocery bag and spread it out on the kitchen table. The front page carried the story about the unidentified man in Corner Brook. "Listen to this," he said, reading aloud. "Police are still trying to learn the identity of a man taken to the Western Memorial Hospital in Corner Brook on Wednesday. They believe the man, estimated to be between 40 and 45 years of age, had been robbed and left in a ditch. The man has blond hair and a scar on his left leg. Anyone with information about his identity is asked to come forward."

"Sure, that's old news now," Leah told him. "I was talking to Mom a little while ago, and she told me the man's family contacted the hospital. They've arranged to have him flown back to the United States as soon as he's well enough."

"An American?" Colin said. "Did your mother find out his name?"

"I didn't ask. I doubt she even knows. What difference does it make?"

"That man could be Dad," Colin said. "It all fits, his age, the hair color, the scar on his leg. And he was… is American."

Leah stared at him. "But wouldn't your mother go to see him? Corner Brook is only a couple of hours away."

"Things have changed between them," Colin said, a catch in his voice. "I don't think they care about each other anymore." He told Leah about the fight his parents had before Dad left for Kenya. "I think they may be getting a divorce."

"I'm sorry." Leah lightly touched his arm.

"What's worse is not knowing if it's Dad in that hospital bed."

"It does seem like a weird coincidence," Leah said. "The description fits. The scar on his leg is the most telling. Mom said it was strange that no one came to see the man after his identity was revealed." She furrowed her brow, as if trying to remember something. "I think Mom said he was some kind of government official."

"Dad's a diplomat," Colin said. He turned so he was facing Leah. "Is there a bus that goes to Corner Brook?"

Leah stared at him. "You're not planning to—"

"I need to see my father and make sure he's okay."

"They won't allow you on the bus without a parent's consent."

A few moments of silence passed between them. "We'll go to Corner Brook together," Leah said with determination. "It's not fair that you don't know where your father is. And I need to see Mom."

"But how will we get there?"

"We'll go with Uncle Eli. He's heading for Port-aux-Basques tonight."

"Will he mind?"

Leah grinned. "He can't mind if he doesn't know we're traveling with him, now can he?" She pointed to the window where a half-ton truck was parked in the driveway. "We'll stow away in the back of his truck."

"But how will *I* get away?" Colin asked. "I can't very well sneak out of the academy in the middle of the night."

"Wait here," Leah instructed. "I'm going to speak to Aunt Flo and your mom."

"But…"

"Trust me," she said, heading for the door.

No one seemed to notice Leah as she walked across the yard. John, their neighbor, was strumming softly on a guitar. Eli was busy minding the barbeque. Granny was talking to an American couple who were staying with some neighbors. "I still thinks the election of 1949 was all a sham," Leah heard her say.

Leah sat down next to Aunt Flo. Colin's mother sat across from them. "Leah, my love," Aunt Flo said. "I was wondering were you went." She looked around the yard. "Where's Colin to?"

"He's inside."

"You left him inside by his own self?"

"He's resting."

"Is he okay?" Catherine asked.

"Just tired." Leah looked from Aunt Flo back to Catherine. "That's why he didn't go camping with Jason and Brent. He knew they'd be awake half the night, and he's worn out from lack of sleep."

"Oh, the poor youngster," Aunt Flo said.

"He says it's noisy at the academy," Leah continued. "Colin finds it hard to sleep."

"He didn't mention anything to me," Catherine said. She looked concerned.

Leah shrugged. "What good would it do to complain? It's not like he can go home. Can't even check into a motel, sure."

Catherine frowned. "There's a little girl in our room who wakes up two and three times a night. Some of the other kids wake up too." She shook her head. "It's starting to take its toll on me. I should have realized it was affecting Colin, too."

"He'll probably be worn out by the time he gets back to New York," Leah said.

"No reason why he can't sleep in Brent's bed tonight," Aunt Flo said. "Brent and Jason are sleeping in a tent."

"We don't want to put you to any trouble," Catherine said. "You've already been so kind to us."

"No trouble at all, my dear," Aunt Flo said. "A good night's sleep will do wonders for that poor youngster."

Leah grinned. It was exactly what she had expected Aunt Flo to say.

Chapter 22

Unable to sleep, Rabia turned on the light, and reached for her envelope of photographs. She found it comforting to look at the pictures of her family. She was glad now that she had smuggled them out of Afghanistan. As long as she had their pictures, she would never forget what Amir, Yousef, and Father looked like. She would take the photos down to the kitchen, she decided, where she could spread them out on the table.

Millie and Kevin were sitting on the sofa in the family room. The television was on, the sound muted. On the screen was a picture of the smoldering rubble at Ground Zero. Firemen and rescue workers were still searching for people who might be trapped in the debris. From the landing, Rabia watched the image change to footage shot in Afghanistan. Women wearing burqas were walking in the street. More and more now, Afghanistan was in the news. Her country had been ignored for years, but now the whole world was paying attention.

"If President Bush goes to war with Afghanistan, it will bring more death and destruction to innocent people," she heard Kevin say.

Rabia gasped, and Kevin and Millie turned to stare at her. So, it *was* true. The president *was* planning an attack. She tried to swallow the panic that rose in her throat.

"Rabia, my love," Millie said. "Come sit with us. Would you like some tea? A glass of milk?"

"Thank you. No," Rabia said. She crossed the room, and sat on a love seat across from them. "Will Americans destroy Afghanistan?"

Millie gave her a pitying look.

Kevin got up from the sofa and came to sit beside Rabia. He took her hand in his briefly. "Bush will go to war," he said. "That much is fairly certain. But I seriously doubt they will bomb the whole country."

Rabia met his gaze. "No?"

Kevin stroked his gray beard. "The best thing the Americans can do is drive Al-Qaeda and the Taliban out of the country. The president should step up to the plate and help Afghans build a stable government. It would be in the best interest of the Americans to do that."

Something in Kevin's tone suggested he did not trust the American president to get things right.

But Rabia felt a wave of hope. If the Taliban were driven from Afghanistan, it would be good for everyone. Her eyes flickered back to the television. "Woman would no longer have to wear the burqa," she said, speaking her thoughts aloud.

"Is that what they calls them outfits?" Millie turned her gaze to the screen. "I can't imagine walking around all day long rigged up like that. Looks like mummers, sure."

The image on the television changed to towering rugged mountains in Kabul.

"Tis a beautiful country," Millie said, turning to look at Rabia. "Reminds me of Newfoundland in some ways."

"Yes, beautiful," Rabia agreed, feeling a wave of homesickness.

Kevin gave her an encouraging smile. "This could be the beginning of something better for Afghanistan," he said. "The country could go back to the way it was under King Khan."

Rabia glanced up at him, surprised he knew about the history of her country. King Amanullah Khan was Afghanistan's first modern ruler. He won independence from Britain in 1919, and started the first school for girls. Like Father, King Khan believed girls should be educated.

Rabia placed the envelope of photographs on a long low table in front of the sofa. "Afghans...we only want freedom."

Kevin nodded. "It's hard to live without freedom."

"And we thinks we got it bad here," Millie said, shaking her head. She looked at Rabia. "What do you have in the envelope?"

"Pictures."

"Of your family?"

"I show you." Rabia took the pictures from the envelope, and spread them out on the table. "Mama... she took a lot of pictures."

"Is she a photographer?" Millie asked.

Rabia nodded. "Yes. Photographer."

Millie picked up a print from the table and studied it.

"Karim," Rabia said. In the photo, he was about six years old. He was staring into the camera, a mischievous grin on his face.

"Is that Karim?" A look of sadness passed over Millie's face. "Sure, you'd never guess it was the same youngster." She put down the photograph, picked up another. "And who are these handsome young men?"

"My brothers. Amir and Yousef. And this is my

father." Rabia held up a picture of a smiling man standing in front of a mosque.

"What happened to your father?" Kevin asked.

In a trembling voice, Rabia told them about the day the Taliban arrested him. "We have not heard from him since. We do not know where he is."

Kevin and Millie exchanged looks of horror. "How did you escape?" Kevin asked.

Rabia explained about the letter that came from her aunt in Quetta. She told them about their journey to Pakistan to apply for the program that would allow them to go to America.

"My," Millie said, shaking her head. "You're some brave, my dear. I don't think I would've had the courage."

"Was it difficult to get into the program?" Kevin asked.

"Yes, difficult," Rabia said, "very difficult. Many, many refugees came to register. It was so crowded, but my foot saved me." Rabia smiled at the memory.

"I can see why they'd pick a handicapped child," Millie said.

Rabia shook her head. "There were many worse than me."

"Oh?" said Kevin.

Rabia told them about her prosthesis falling off, about nearly being trampled.

"It's a wonder you weren't killed," Millie said.

Rabia nodded. "I thought I would die."

Kevin was looking at her with admiration. "You were lucky," he said.

"Yes," Rabia said. "I am very lucky." At the time, she felt the way she imagined Jack must have felt when he won passage on the *Titanic*. But now she could not help wondering if she was doomed to the same kind of fate.

Chapter 23

Leah was still grinning when she walked back to the house. *What's she up to?* Colin wondered as he watched from the window.

"It's all settled," she said, bursting into the kitchen. "You're going to sleep in Brent's room tonight."

"Mom agreed?" Colin's jaw dropped. What on earth could Leah have said to convince Mom and Aunt Flo to let him spend the night?

"You'll need to go back to the academy to get some of your things."

"Yes," Colin agreed. He'd need a change of clothing, at least.

"We have sleeping bags," Leah said. "And hot-water bottles to put inside. We'll need a flashlight. Bottled

145

water." She went to the cupboard and found pop, chips, dip, and cookies.

Colin smiled. The trip was starting to have the feel of an adventure. Leah was still adding to the list when Uncle Eli came into the house.

"You're missing all the fun," he said, "and all the great steaks and hamburgers I barbequed."

"We have to go to the academy," Leah said. "We'll eat later."

"Food will be cold by then. I already turned off the grill."

"What time are you leaving in the morning?" Leah asked, her voice casual.

"Around two a.m. Always good to be early." Eli took off his jacket and hung it in the closet. "The ferries could shut down if Hurricane Erin has her way."

Colin shot Leah a worried look. Erin was the first major storm of the season. There was concern it would make landfall in the States. He was surprised it was expected in Newfoundland.

"This could ruin our plans," Colin whispered as Eli turned and walked down the hallway to his bedroom.

Leah looked at her list. "In any case, we should be prepared."

On the way to the academy Leah laid out her plan. They would put most of their things in the truck before going to bed. Her alarm was set to go off at midnight. By the time, Uncle Eli got up they would already be in the truck. She would leave a note on her bureau. By the time the note was discovered, she would have already phoned Aunt Flo from Corner Brook. The only problem Leah could see was Granny. The old lady stayed awake all hours of the night, writing letters and reading detective novels borrowed from the library.

"Whenever Uncle Eli goes to Corner Brook, he stops at Kate's Kitchen," Leah told Colin. "It's an all night diner where truck drivers and mill workers eat. I'll take my alarm clock. Set it for four a.m., an hour before he should get there. When he stops, we'll get out of the truck and head for the hospital."

By the time they arrived back at the house, most of the guests had gone home, and the bonfire had burned to ash. Granny and Catherine had their chairs pulled close together. "What charm those American soldiers had," Granny was saying. "My dear, all the young girls fell madly in love with them. Our local men were right jealous."

Granny stopped talking when Colin and Leah came into the yard. "There they are now," she said.

Catherine stood up. "I should get back to the school before dark." She kissed Colin's cheek. "Try to get a good night's rest. I'll see you in the morning."

"Okay, Mom," Colin said, feeling a tug of guilt. No doubt, she'd be upset when she found out he was gone. What if it triggered one of her headaches?

Back in the house, Aunt Flo came down the hallway, her arms loaded with sheets. "Your room's ready," she told him. "I know you must be eager to get some sleep."

Colin gave her an odd look. He never went to bed this early.

"I told her you were tired." Leah explained after Aunt Flo was out of earshot. "Anyway, it might be a good idea for us to go to bed early. We have to get up at midnight."

Leah showed him to a small, cramped room with barely enough space to hold a narrow bed and a scratched bureau. There was no television or computer, not even a telephone. A couple of library books sat on the bureau. The room could have fit inside the walk-in closet of his New York bedroom.

The walls were bare except for a large map — a map of Gander. An identical one hung in the classroom at the academy. From the moment Colin saw the map, he knew there was something odd about it. Now, he saw that the streets of the town were arranged to resemble a gander — a male goose. *Cool,* Colin thought, tracing his finger along part of the neck that formed Memorial Drive. *What a neat idea.*

He turned down the handmade quilt and switched off the light. For a long time, he tossed and turned in the darkness. Switching the lamp back on, he reached into his knapsack for his game and inserted the new battery he'd bought earlier, but his thoughts were on Rabia. He felt badly for being so rude to her. She had grown up in a war zone, had her foot blown off by a landmine. She had lost her father, her brother, and her country. Now, she might lose her mother. Mom was right: the terrorist attack was not her fault. Her family was coming to America to get away from terrorists and to start a new life, not to wage war.

An alien appeared on the screen and Colin blew it away, but it gave him no satisfaction. He was bored with the silly game. For months, he'd played the stupid thing, going from level to level. What a waste of time. He put it on the bureau, turned out the light, and tried to sleep.

• • •

A soft but persistent knock on the bedroom door interrupted Colin's restless sleep. "Colin, get up!" Leah whispered into the crack. "Uncle Eli will be awake soon."

Groggy with sleep, Colin got out of bed and groped his way into the kitchen. Leah handed him a hot-water bottle. "I've already filled it," she told him.

Outside, rain danced on the roof and spit against the windows. Leah held up a raincoat. "It belongs to Brent," she said. "It should fit."

It was twenty past twelve by the time they climbed into the back of Eli's tuck. Despite the hard floor, Colin had no trouble getting back to sleep. He didn't even stir when the truck began to move. He woke some time later, confused and disorientated. Music was coming from somewhere. For a moment, he wondered if he was dreaming. But slowly, everything came back to him. Then he realized the truck wasn't moving.

Leah," he whispered. "Wake up. I think we're in Corner Brook."

Leah moaned and turned over. "What time is it?"

Colin looked at his watch. "Almost 3 a.m."

"It's too early to be in Corner Brook." Leah crawled out of her sleeping bag, and looked through the tiny curtained window on the side of the truck. "Looks like some kind of night club."

Colin joined her at the window. "I need to go to the bathroom," he said. "There must be one inside."

They pulled on their raincoats and climbed down from the truck. As they made their way to the building, gusts of wind blew rain in their faces. A man and woman came through the door as they were about to go in. "Where are we?" Leah asked them.

"The Holy Grail," the man said, pointing to a sign above the tavern door.

"What's the name of the town?"

The woman gave her an odd look. "You're in Badger, my love." She frowned. "Kind of late for youngsters to be hanging around a bar."

"We need to use the bathroom," Leah said.

"You have to go down a flight of steps," the woman told her. "They don't allow youngsters, but I s'pose they won't mind you using the bathroom."

Leah thanked her, and she and Colin moved into a small foyer. A poster of three smiling women was taped to the wall. In the dim light, he could barely make out the words written beneath it:

The Sirous Sisters
Playing at the Holy Grail Tavern
in Badger on Friday, September 14.
Come join Lucy, Hailey, and Olivia
and make beautiful music together!

"Uncle Eli loves the Sirous Sisters," Leah said. "He'd stay here forever if he could."

Poking his head in the door, Colin saw people dancing in a small open space in front of the bandstand. Even from here, smoke burned his eyes and throat. "There's Uncle Eli," Leah said. "He's dancing over there." Eli swung around the dance floor, holding onto a girl in a red dress.

"C'mon," Leah said, giving Colin a nudge. "If Uncle Eli sees us, he'll march us straight back to Gander."

After using the bathroom, they ran for the truck and crawled back inside their sleeping bags.

Colin fretted and tossed in his sleep. New York was on fire and he was trying to flee the burning city with his father. In the distance he could hear the wail of sirens.

"Colin, wake up."

Colin's eyes flew open. Leah was beside him. He was surprised that he could still hear the sirens. "What's going on?" he asked groggily, as the truck came to a stop.

"The police," Leah said. She went to kneel by the window and Colin joined her. It was getting light now, and the rain had eased to a drizzle.

They watched as an officer got out of the cruiser and approached Eli. From inside the truck, Colin and Leah could hear Eli. "I didn't know it was broken, sir. I'll get it fixed first chance I gets."

The officer said something they couldn't make out.

"It's in the back," Eli said. "Give me a minute now, and I'll go get it."

Leah and Colin exchanged looks. Eli was walking around the back of the truck. "Oh, no," Leah said, as the back door creaked open.

Eli stared at them a long moment, a stunned look on his face. "Leah? Colin? What the…"

Chapter 24

It was still dark outside when Millie knocked on Rabia's bedroom door. "My dear, time to get up," she called.

Rabia was already awake. She had been awake most of the night, thinking about Mama.

"I will come soon," she called through the closed door. She got out of bed and dressed quickly.

Karim was already sitting at the breakfast table when she went into the kitchen. Millie had cooked eggs and pancakes. Rabia smiled at her brother. "We are going to see Mama today, Karim."

He gave her a blank stare. *Does he know what is going on?* Rabia wondered. *Does he miss Mama the way I do?*

Last night, Millie and Kevin had explained their plan. They would return to Gander that evening. Karim and Rabia would stay in Corner Brook with Millie's cousin Joy, whose mother was in the same hospital recovering from an operation. Joy would stay with them in the hostel and care for them until they were ready to return to Gander.

"Did you get in touch with your caseworker?" Kevin asked when he came into the kitchen.

Rabia shook her head. "I was not able to reach her." Fatima had called Rabia while she and Karim were out on the boats. Rabia had tried to reach her a number of times but kept getting her voice mail.

"Why don't we try again now?" Kevin said.

Rabia looked at him. It was still very early in California; Fatima would probably be sleeping.

"This *is* an emergency," Kevin said, as if reading her thoughts. "She should know what's going on. I can try the number for you, if you like."

Rabia nodded. "Thank you."

"The number is on the fridge," Millie told him.

Kevin punched in the number. The answering machine must have come on because he left his name and phone number. He also left a number where Fatima could reach them at the hospital. "It's an emergency," he said, signing off.

Rabia felt a surge of gratitude; it felt good having an adult take charge. Being with Millie and Kevin felt like the time before Father went away. Before Mama lost interest in everything, and Rabia's world still felt safe.

It was not yet six a.m. when they boarded the van. As they drove down the tree-lined streets, Rabia could not help comparing it to Kabul. Girls and women were free to go outside whenever they felt like it. They wore trousers, flaunted tattoos, and had body parts, including their bellybuttons, pierced. Rabia had even seen one girl who had shaved her head. None of them ever had to worry about being beaten by Taliban thugs. *This is what it's like to be free,* Rabia thought.

After a while the car pulled onto the main road, and all Rabia could see were trees and bushes. The car radio was playing music, and although she did not understand the words, it made her happy.

When the music stopped, a newscaster came on. "People whose flights were diverted because of the attack on the World Trade Center in New York City may be able to fly to their destinations as early as this evening. Passengers are being told to be ready at a moment's notice. It has been four days now since the terrorist attack, and people have been stranded all across Canada."

"No," Rabia said, causing Kevin to turn and look at her. "We will miss the plane!" Rabia's voice was shaky.

"There will be other planes, sure," said Millie.

Rabia shook her head. "We have no money for tickets."

"I'm sure something can be arranged," Kevin said, encouragingly. "Maybe the airlines will change your tickets at no extra cost. It's not your fault the plane was diverted. I'll look into it when I get back to work," he promised.

Rabia breathed easier. Somehow Kevin always managed to make things right.

They had been driving for about half an hour when she saw the strange creature come out of the bushes. It was huge with large horns coming from its head. "Look!" Rabia shouted.

"That's a moose," Millie told her. "They're common around here. Sure, last summer one came down the main street in Gander. Tried to walk into the grocery store."

"Moose," Rabia repeated, a note of fear in her voice.

"Don't worry, my dear," Millie said. "They're right tame, mostly. More frightened of us then we are of them."

The animal was enormous. Rabia would not want to meet a moose while she was alone. She leaned back in the seat, and closed her eyes.

• • •

Rabia awoke with a start. They were just passing a sign that said, Welcome to Corner Brook.

"We're here," Millie announced.

Rabia looked at the city sprawled below. Houses sloped toward an oval harbor, the buildings perched crazily against mountains and hills. It looked like it had started out as a village that had suddenly grown out of control.

Kevin pulled the car onto a street called East Valley Road. After a few minutes, he stopped in front of a large red brick building. *This must be where they have brought Mama,* Rabia thought. Unexpectedly, she burst into tears.

Chapter 25

Eli continued to stare at Colin and Leah, a stunned look on his face.

"We needed a ride to Corner Brook," Leah said lamely.

Eli shook his head. "All I needs now." He glared at Leah. "Bet Aunt Flo don't know where you're to." He shifted his gaze to Colin. "And Colin, my son, I'm surprised at you. What if the airport calls while you're here? Planes could leave any time now. Yeh mother's probably worried sick."

"I left a note for Aunt Flo." Leah explained.

Eli sighed. "I'll drop you off at Debbie's."

"Mom's working," Leah said. "She gets off work in…" She glanced at her watch, "…in about an hour."

"All right," Eli said, "I'll drop you off at the hospital."

Colin's heart began to beat faster. If things went as planned, he'd see Dad soon.

Half an hour later, Eli pulled the truck in front of the hospital's main entrance. "I'll call Debbie," he said. "Let her know you're here. Wait in the cafeteria."

After Uncle Eli drove off, Leah glanced at her watch. "We have about forty-five minutes," she told Colin. "Mom's friend works in the gift shop. She might know something."

Leah led Colin through the hospital's main entrance, and straight to the gift shop. A woman in a pale blue uniform was dusting glass display cases. "Leah?" she said. "Debbie said you weren't coming this weekend."

"There…uh…there's been a change of plans." Leah looked at Colin. "Colin, this is Mom's friend Paula."

"Hi, Colin." Paula gave him a warm smile.

"Pleased to meet you, ma'am," he said.

"Anything I can help you with?"

"Mom told me about the man the police brought here on Wednesday evening," Leah said, fishing for information.

Paula shook her head, sadly. "Poor fellar. None of his family came to visit."

Colin felt terrible. *I'm coming to visit you now, Dad*, he promised silently.

"At least he's out of the intensive care unit and down to the third floor now," Paula said. "That's a good sign, anyway."

Colin and Leah exchanged glances.

A customer came into the shop and Paula went to see if he needed help. Leah grabbed Colin's hand and pulled him outside. "He's probably in the room across from the nurses' station," she said.

"How do you know that?"

"Mom said whenever patients leave the ICU they put them near the nurses' station so they can keep a close eye on them." She led Colin to a bank of elevators. "Let's go find out."

The elevator stopped at the third floor and they got off. At this early hour the corridor was empty. "I'll wait here," Leah said, taking a seat on an upholstered bench.

Colin crept down the hallway until he came to a horseshoe-shaped desk. A nurse was reading a chart. Across from the desk was room 312. The nurse didn't look up as Colin sneaked past. Heart pounding, he pushed open the door and stepped inside. The curtains were drawn and the room was dim, but Colin could make out tubes and bags hooked to the man in the bed. He approached quietly, and put his a hand on the man's shoulder.

The patient opened his eyes and stared at Colin, fear

etched on his face. "Agggh!" he cried out, flinging his arms.

It's not Dad, Colin realized, backing away. *I'm in the wrong room.* The man continued to yell.

A nurse charged into the room. "What's going on?" she demanded, rushing to the patient's side.

"He's not Dad," Colin said, stupidly.

He was backing out of the room when an orderly came in. "Everything okay?" he asked, his eyes darting from Colin to the nurse. The patient had quieted down, but was clutching the blankets, terrified.

The nurse glared at Colin. "Call security," she told the orderly.

• • •

"I went into the wrong room," Colin told Sam, the aging security guard sitting across from him. He had been ushered from the hospital room like a criminal. Now, he and Leah sat in a small office waiting for Leah's mother.

"Who were you looking for?" Sam's blue eyes bore into Colin.

"William Erickson. My father. He was brought here by the police on Thursday."

"Only one man was brought here by the police," the

guard said, patiently. "The one you just nearly scared to death."

"You mean…" Colin paled as the guard's words sank in.

"There's no William Erickson registered at this hospital, son."

Colin stared at him. *Had he come all this way for nothing? But where was Dad? He should have arrived in Newfoundland on Wednesday.*

A knock at the door startled him.

"Please, come in," Sam said.

Leah's mom stepped into the room, wearing a white sweater over her uniform, her dark hair pinned back from her face. "Leah, for heaven's sake," she said. "What's going on? First, Eli calls saying you stowed away in his truck. Now this."

"I'm sorry, Mom," Leah said. "I was helping Colin look for his dad."

Debbie shook her head, her gaze falling on Colin. "Colin," she said, her tone softening, "why would you think your father is here?"

Colin couldn't speak. He had expected to find Dad here. The disappointment was like a slammed door.

Debbie turned to Sam. "I'm sorry about this," she said. "Are they free to go?"

Sam shrugged. "Okay by me."

Debbie stood up. "Let's go to the cafeteria," she said, "and try to sort this out."

Colin and Leah followed her down the hallway to the elevators. "Why did you think you'd find your father in Mr. Cooper's room?" she asked Colin.

"I'm sorry I upset him," Colin said, his voice trembling. He told her about the phone calls he'd made to New York the morning after the attack. "Dad was in New York, yet Mom let me believe he was still in Kenya." Colin toyed with the zipper on his jacket. "Later, I found out Dad was on his way to Newfoundland to be with us. He didn't show. When I found out about the man the police brought here, I figured he was Dad. Scar on his left leg, the same hair color — everything."

The elevator doors slid open, and they got on. "You never discussed *any* of this with your mother?" Debbie asked.

"No," Colin admitted, feeling foolish. "But she kept things from me, too."

Debbie shook her head. "There could've been a dozen reasons why your mom didn't tell you about your dad. It would've been wise to talk to her before coming here."

"That was partly my fault," Leah said, lowering her eyes. "I discouraged him from talking to his mother."

Debbie gave her daughter a curious look. "Why

164

would you do that?"

"I thought she was keeping things from Colin. The way you and Aunt Flo kept things from Brent and me after Dad died."

Debbie stared at her.

"I had to find out from Jenny Payne what happened to him."

The elevator stopped. "We were trying to protect you," Debbie said, as they stepped out into the hallway. She shook her head sadly. "I guess that was wrong. And to be honest, I don't know if it was you I was trying to protect, or myself."

"I should have talked to Mom," Colin said.

Debbie handed him her cell phone. "It's not too late. Call her. She knows you're here, but I'm sure she'd appreciate hearing from you. And you can tell her you'll be back late tonight. Eli said he was leaving here this evening and would take you back to Gander with him."

"Thank you," Colin said, accepting the phone.

"We'll meet you in the cafeteria."

Colin punched in his mother's number.

"Colin, thank God," she said when she answered. "I've been worried sick."

"I'm sorry I worried you, Mom," he said. "I came here hoping to find Dad." He told her about the phone call to Ed Nestor.

"Your father's in New York, Colin. On special assignment. He *was* planning to come for us, but then he was asked not to leave because of everything that was happening. I didn't tell you he'd returned from Kenya because I thought it would be a nice surprise when you got home."

Colin felt a wave of relief. His dad was safe. He would see him shortly. "Eli is leaving this evening. He says I can ride back with him."

"Let's hope you get here before the airport calls. Some planes have left already." Catherine sighed. "Colin, do you really believe if your father was lying in a hospital I wouldn't go see him? Do you think I'd keep something like that from you?"

"Well…you and Dad haven't been getting along."

"True," she agreed, after a long pause. "But things are about to change."

Change. "Why is that?" Colin asked anxiously.

"We'll talk about it when we get home."

"Right," Colin muttered. But his dad was safe. He would see him soon. That was all that mattered right now.

Chapter 26

"Mama," Rabia whispered, inching closer to the hospital bed. "Mama? Can you hear me?"

Mama's eyes fluttered open, briefly. She had been moved from the intensive care unit, but she was bound to the bed by tubes and monitors. She looked so small and frail against the hospital sheets that Rabia had to blink back tears.

A nurse, who had been standing by the window filling in a chart, came to stand by the bed. "Your mother should be out of here in a week," she said. "She's doing really well. It was only a mild attack, not nearly as bad as we first thought."

Rabia felt a surge of relief. Nothing was more important than Mama's health. It was as if a weight attached to her own heart had suddenly been cut loose. "Did you hear, Karim?" She whispered. "Mama is going to be all right."

Mama's eyes opened again, and she stared at Rabia. Rabia squeezed her hand. "Everything is going to be fine, Mama." Her mother's lips moved. "What is it, Mama?" Rabia asked, leaning toward her.

Mama's voice was so soft, she had to strain to hear. "Thank you, Rabia."

"For what, Mama?"

"You are a good daughter." Mama's voice was weak. "I always thought it would be my sons...my sons who would take care of me. But daughter, you are brave and courageous."

"Oh, Mama," Rabia said, holding back her tears.

"I do not know," Mama continued, "how I could have managed...without you. Your...father would be very proud."

Rabia could no longer hold back her tears. She had waited all her life for her mother to say something like this. Mama's words meant so much to her. She felt as if she had been handed a precious gift.

"You should go now," the nurse told them. "Your mother needs her rest."

"I will come back and see you again, Mama," Rabia said, tucking the blankets around her. She reached for her brother's hand.

Kevin stood up when Rabia walked into the lobby. "What's wrong?" he asked, concern clouding his face. "Is your mother okay?"

"Mama will be fine," Rabia said. "She will have to stay here for a week."

"That's not long, sure," Millie said. "Not for someone who suffered a heart attack."

"Your caseworker called a few minutes ago," said Kevin. "Called the front desk. She wants you to phone her back." He pointed to a payphone on the wall. "Use the one over there."

Kevin dialed the operator and told her he wanted to make a collect call. After rattling off Fatima's number, he handed the receiver to Rabia.

Fatima picked up on the first ring. "Hello, Fatima," Rabia said in Dari.

"Rabia, I am glad you called. I'm so sorry to hear about your mother. How is she doing?"

Rabia explained that Mama would be in the hospital for another week. "The planes will be gone then."

"Don't worry about that, Rabia," Fatima said. "As soon as your mother is able to travel, we will take care of your tickets. You are our responsibility now. I do not want you fretting about such things."

Rabia closed her eyes, a wave of relief washing over her; it was one less thing to worry about. But there was something else, and she might as well ask about it right now. "Fatima," she said, "I heard that the relief organization is Christian. Will we be able to practice our faith in America?"

"Of course," Fatima said. "I am free to practice my faith any way I choose. The people who run this organization only want to help people have a better life."

"I am so glad to hear that, Fatima."

"But Rabia," Fatima said, and Rabia could hear the concern in her voice. "This is not a good time to be a Muslim in America."

Rabia swallowed, waiting for her to continue.

"People are angry," Fatima said. "They blame us for the destruction of the World Trade Center. People are afraid of us."

"I heard on television that they have threatened Muslims," Rabia said quietly. "They have attacked mosques."

"They are judging all of us by the actions of extremists." Fatima paused as if considering what to say next. "People will get over this, Rabia. They need time."

"Yes," Rabia agreed, but she could not help worrying.

"Let me know how your mother is doing," Fatima said before she signed off.

"Yes, I will," Rabia agreed. "Good-bye, Fatima. Thank you."

"Everything okay?" Millie asked when Rabia got off the phone.

"Fatima said not to worry about the plane."

"There now, you see, my love? That's good news."

Rabia nodded. She looked at Millie and sighed. "I wish we could stay here...in Canada."

Millie met her gaze. "Why is that, my dear?"

"Americans...they do not like us. They do not understand."

"Why do you say that?"

"They attack mosques..." Rabia searched for the right English words. "In Canada it is different. People understand."

Millie stared at her a long moment before she spoke. "Don't yeh think Kevin understands your situation?"

Rabia glanced at Kevin, who had been listening to their conversation. He gave her a small, sad smile. Why was Millie asking her this? *Of course, Kevin understands. Next to Father, Kevin is the kindest man I know.*

"Kevin's from Boston," Millie said. "Came from the States in 1996. We got married the following year."

It took Rabia a moment to realize what Millie was saying. "Kevin is American?"

Millie laughed. "Can't yeh tell by the funny way he talks?"

Rabia felt the blood rush to her cheeks. She was

horrified. She had insulted Kevin who had been so good to her. He and Millie had taken her into their home. What must he think of her? She felt so ashamed she could not even look at him. And worst, she had assumed that *all* Americans were against her. Only minutes ago, she had been trying to understand why Americans assumed *all* Muslims were terrorists.

"Sorry," Rabia mumbled, her face burning. She forced herself to look at Kevin, but could not quite meet his eyes. She saw his mouth crinkle into a smile.

"All Americans are not plotting against you," Kevin said. "People are upset. They are looking for someone to blame. But remember, for every American who rejects you, there will be about ten more who will like you just as much as we do."

Rabia met his gaze. "You think?"

Kevin nodded. "You are going to do just fine in America, Rabia." He stood up. "Now let's go find the cafeteria. I'm starving."

Chapter 27

"Well, my, my. Look who's here," Millie said, when they walked into the cafeteria.

Rabia followed her gaze to a long table where Leah was sitting with a nurse. "Hi Rabia," she called brightly as they approached. She turned to the woman beside her. "Mom, this is Rabia and Karim."

Smiling, Debbie reached for Rabia's hand. "Sorry to hear about your mother," she said. "How is she?"

"Mama…she is getting better."

"Should be out of the hospital in a few days," Millie offered.

"Would you like to hang out with us?" Leah asked.

"Hang…?"

"We're going downtown. You and Karim can come along if you like."

"Why don't you go with them, my love," Millie said. "Sure, it'll do yeh good to get away from this place for a little while."

"Yes," Rabia agreed eagerly. "We will go."

At that moment, Colin came into the cafeteria. Rabia's mouth fell open. What was that American boy doing here? She watched as he walked toward them. He handed Leah's mother a phone. "Thank you, Mrs. Pickford."

"Did you get through okay?"

"Yes. I talked with Mom."

"Rabia and Karim are going to come downtown with us," Leah told him.

Rabia took a step backward.

Colin turned to her. "I was sorry to hear about your mother," he said.

Rabia eyed him warily. How did he know about Mama?

"Well," Leah said, buttoning her jacket. "Let's get out of here."

Rabia hesitated, but she followed after them.

The hospital was built on a hill overlooking the city. From where she stood Rabia could see into the leafy backyards of houses below. Birds huddled together on clotheslines and telephone wires. The rain had stopped, and the sun was struggling to pierce the dark low clouds.

Rabia felt a lightness in her step. Mama had called her brave. Mama was proud of her. She wanted to shout it out to the world.

Leah led the way down the steep hill, chattering continually as she walked. She told Rabia about how she and Colin stowed away in the back of her uncle's truck.

Rabia listened, fascinated. Leah's life was so different from her own.

They made their way down the hill until they came to West Valley Road. From there they walked all the way to West Street. Leah and Rabia walked ahead while Colin and Karim lagged behind. Shops, restaurants, drugstores, and office buildings lined the street. The spicy aroma of chicken wafted through the damp air. Rabia stopped to admire the mannequins in store windows. There were men and woman as well as child-sized figures. They looked like real people with blond, red, and dark hair. When the Taliban came to Kabul, they lopped the heads off all the store mannequins.

"Let's rest," Leah said, leading Rabia to a bench beside a picnic table in a grassy clearing off the main street. Across from them was a sagging building that looked ready to fall down. The roof had caved in, and all the windows were broken. It reminded Rabia of the bombed out buildings in Kabul. A sign in front said, **Danger: No Trespassing.** But Rabia could not read the English words. The house looked out of place among the trees and flowers and tidy buildings.

"Before he died, my dad used to take me into the city all the time," Leah said. "He grew up in Corner Brook."

Rabia saw Colin and Karim heading toward the old building. "Your father...how did he die?"

"There was a fire in a building he was working on. He didn't make it out," Leah said sadly. "That was about three years ago." She looked at Rabia. "What happened to *your* father?"

"I do not know," Rabia answered. She told Leah about how the Taliban had come to their house and dragged him away.

"They can just do that?" Leah asked, her eyes wide. "That's horrible."

"Yes," Rabia said, sadly. "Is horrible."

Leah looked toward the sky. "Still, in a way I envy you."

"Envy?" Rabia repeated. Out of the corner of her eye, she saw Colin climb up on the verandah of the abandoned house.

"Sometimes I dream about my dad," Leah said. "I wake up and realize he's never coming back." Her eyes grew sad. "You still have hope that your dad will return."

Rabia briefly touched her arm. "Yes," she nodded. "Still hope."

Father used to say that hope chased away despair. Rabia thought of her neighbors and relatives back in Afghanistan. Even though they were in desperate situations, they still held hope that things would get better. Leah was right. Hope made it possible to believe that anything could happen.

Rabia was so lost in her thoughts she did not notice the black-and-white car pull up on the street across from them. Its door slammed, jolting her out of her musings. The car had a row of red and blue lights on top. Two men were approaching them. They wore uniforms with blue stripes down the legs of their trousers. One was no older than Yousef. He was skinny with a mustache. The other, an older man, had streaks of silver in his hair. Police. Rabia glanced quickly at Karim and Colin. Both boys were on the verandah of the house now.

"You know those kids?" the older officer asked, his gaze straying to the abandoned building.

"My brother," Rabia said, feeling her mouth go dry.

The officer shook his head. "They shouldn't be there. Can't they read the sign?"

Rabia's heart began to race. How could she have been so careless? If the police arrested Karim, he would be taken to prison. Losing another son would kill Mama. They would never get to America. Rabia couldn't bear it. She watched helplessly as the officers approached the boys. The older one beckoned for them to come down from the verandah. *Karim cannot read English,* Rabia wanted to shout. *He does not talk. But he is a good boy!*

The police came back to the bench, Colin and Karim in tow. "Where are you kids from?"

"I'm from Gander," Leah said.

"I'm from New York," Colin said. "Karim and Rabia are from Afghanistan."

"Afghanistan," the younger officer said, giving them an odd look. "Did you kids come in on the planes that got diverted to Gander on Tuesday?" He seemed more curious than anything. Still, Rabia was too frightened to speak. Her whole body trembled.

"Yes," Colin said. "I was on my way from London to New York. Rabia and Karim are going to California."

"What are you all doing in Corner Brook?"

"I came to see my mom," Leah said. "She's training to be a nurse at Western Memorial. Rabia and Karim's mother is in the hospital recovering from a heart attack." She glanced at Colin. "And Colin...Colin came with me."

"I hear there's quite the crowd landed there," the officer said, his voice friendly.

"People are sleeping on church pews and on floors of school gyms," Leah said.

"My brother lives in Glenwood," the younger

officer said. "They have a family from Florida staying with them."

Rabia listened to the conversation, not quite believing it was as friendly as it sounded. Leah spoke with the men as easily as if they were uncles or brothers.

The older officer studied Rabia. "No harm done, young lady. I hope your mother is feeling better soon," he said. "Enjoy your stay in Newfoundland."

"Thank you," Rabia said, stunned that a policeman would say such a thing.

"Why don't you go down to Mill Brook Mall," the younger man suggested. "They have a Lego building marathon going on. I was there yesterday with my nephew. Kids are building all kinds of neat things." He looked pointedly at Colin and Karim. "A lot safer than climbing on top of old buildings."

Rabia watched them walk away, and nearly wept with relief. The Taliban would have arrested them. Maybe taken them to jail, beaten them for sure. But these policemen were only concerned about the boys' safety. Relief swept over Rabia and she sank down onto the bench. It took a few minutes until her shaking subsided.

"Anyone up to building Lego?" Leah asked. "Mill Brook Mall is close by."

They walked in silence until they came to long, low

building built alongside a brook. "Doesn't look much like a mall," Colin said.

"Most of the stores are closed now." Leah said, as they walked up a set of concrete steps to the main entrance and went inside. Kids sat at tables building boats, cars, helicopters, and spaceships with colorful bricks. There were more tables filled with displays of churches, hospitals, trains, rockets, and various animals. On one table was a giant hat. On another, a towering giraffe. Photographs of other creations were displayed along the walls.

"We'd like to sign up for the marathon." Leah told a guard standing by the door.

"Eva's in charge of that," he said. "Over by the booth." He pointed to a plump woman in a navy outfit. "Hey Eva," he called. "Some kids here to see yeh."

The woman came toward them, a pair of reading glasses dangling from a chain around her neck. "What school are yeh from?"

"We're not from around here," Leah said. "We're just visiting."

"Usually, we require a letter from your school giving permission to skip classes." Eva shrugged. "Well, nothing's written in stone." She took their names and led them to an empty table in the corner. "After you've finished your project, we'll keep it on display for twenty-four hours. Then we'll dismantle it to make room for others." She pointed to a wall of photographs. "Before we take it apart, we'll take a picture."

"Sounds good," Leah said.

"You can work alone or in groups," Eva said.

"I'd like for us to work together," Leah said. She glanced at Colin who gave a quick nod of agreement.

"Okay," said Eva. "I'll have someone bring your blocks."

Rabia and Karim sat at one end of the table, Leah and Colin at the other. Minutes later, a boy brought several plastic containers filled with pieces of various shapes and sizes. It was the first time Rabia had seen such a thing. Children in Kabul were not encouraged to play.

Eva came back to the table holding a leaflet, which she placed on the table. "Here are some blueprints," she said. "Of course, you can build from your imagination."

Karim picked up a bright yellow piece, the size of a brick. He turned it around in his small hands. It was the first time in over a year Rabia had seen him show an interest in anything.

"Any idea what we can build?" Colin asked.

"We could build a bridge," Rabia suggested, her eyes fixed on her brother. Karim is good at building bridges."

Leah nodded. "Great idea."

"Okay," Colin said. "Let's build a bridge."

September 19, 2001

Dear Colin,

Thank you for your letter. It is so quiet here now that all the plane people have left, and Uncle Eli moved into his own apartment. There are all kinds of rumors about who was in Gander on 9/11. Some say that Michael Jackson arrived here in his private jet. They say he was given a room in one of the motels in town. I know for a fact that it was Clemens Briels we saw in the grocery store. He was staying at Lakewood Academy in Glenwood. Before he left, he drew a picture on the blackboard using crayons and colored chalk. My cousin Jessica goes to that school. She said the principal had the blackboard removed from the wall. It is now in the school library, framed and covered in Plexiglas.

The Rockefeller Foundation in New York is donating fifty thousand dollars worth of computers to the school in Lewisporte. Someone from the foundation was staying at the school. I wish we could have some new computers for our school. Ours are as slow as molasses, and keep breaking down. But Granny says I should be grateful for what I have instead of complaining about what I don't have.

Aunt Millie had a letter from Rabia. They are doing well. I am sending you her address in case you want to write her. Whenever I look at the picture of the bridge we built at Mill Brook Mall, I think of you and Rabia and Karim. I hope to see you all again someday.

Brent, Granny, and Aunt Flo send their love.
Your friend always,
Leah

September 25, 2001

Dear Leah,
Good to hear from you. Thank you for sending me Rabia's address. I often think of her and Karim. I feel sad whenever I think about what they have gone through.

It will be a long time before things get back to normal around here. I still keep my bedroom curtains drawn. I can't bear to look out at Ground Zero and the pile of rubble. In English class, we had to write an essay about where we were on 9/11. The teacher and the students were fascinated about my stay in

Gander, and our little adventure to Corner Brook. I felt a bit guilty about having had such a good time during what was our city's biggest tragedy.

We hardly recognized Dad when he picked us up at the airport. He had grown a beard and was wearing a sloppy shirt and jeans. I heard him tell Mom that he really missed us. Anyway, he is starting another job at the end of the year. His new job doesn't require him to travel so much. He and Mom are getting along a lot better now. They don't fight nearly as much. For a while, I was afraid they might get a divorce.

Dad never gets tired of hearing stories about our stay in Gander. Last evening, he went on the Internet and Googled Salvage. We may be spending our summer vacation there. Mom has already ordered brochures from the Newfoundland Department of Tourism. So, Leah, if everything goes as planned, we will be in Newfoundland this summer.

I would love to see you all again,
Colin

September 28, 2001

Dear Colin:

Thank you for your letter, and your concern for Mama and Karim. We are all well, and getting settled in our little apartment in Monterey. It is pretty here, quiet and peaceful. Still, I wake up from nightmares where I can't get out of Afghanistan, and I am running from the Taliban. And of course, I miss Father, Amir, and Yousef.

Both Mama and I are enrolled in ESL — English as a second language. I have become friends with Teeka, a refugee girl from Africa. I am hoping Mama and Karim will make some friends also.

Karim is seeing a child psychologist. She says he is still in shock, and it will take time for him to heal. But already, he seems much happier. He is obsessed with the butterfly poppy that grows wild near our compound. Whenever he is outside, he wants to pick them. The apartment is filled with them.

Fatima, my caseworker, who is writing this letter for me, says the world is my oyster. I can finish school, go to college, or find a job. I plan to do all those things, but right now I only want for Mama to be happy and for Karim to start speaking again.

There is talk that the Americans are going to remove the Taliban from Afghanistan. That means that Amir can return from Iran. Father will be freed from prison. This news seems too good to be true. But we never stop hoping.

Keep well my friend,
Rabia.

Author's Note

Although the characters in this book are fictional, the plot is based on real events. On September 11, 2001, terrorist flew jets into the twin towers of the World Trade Center in New York City killing thousands of people. As a result, airspace over the United States was shut down, and pilots were ordered to land at the nearest available airport.

Thirty-eight planes carrying 6,595 passengers were diverted to Gander, Newfoundland, a town with a population of barely 10,000. The community came together to offer food, aid, shelter, and comfort to the stranded passengers.

In 2011, two large pieces of a steel girder from the fallen skyscrapers arrived in Gander to mark the tenth anniversary of that tragic day. The steel is now part of a memorial at the town's North Atlantic Aviation Museum. Many of the stranded airline passengers have returned to Gander in the intervening years to maintain friendships made during those troubled days and to thank the people of Gander for their kindness.

Acknowledgments

I would like to acknowledge with gratitude the support of my friends and fellow writers, Sharon Palermo, Deannie Sullivan Fraser, Barbara Mosher, and Tyne Brown. Thanks also to Kathryn Cole and Carolyn Jackson for their meticulous editing. Finally, a special thank you to my family, Dennis, Christine, and Darcy Walsh for their ongoing love and support.

About the Author

Alice Walsh grew up in northern Newfoundland and now lives in Lower Sackville, Nova Scotia. She writes fiction and nonfiction for adults and children, and her articles and short stories have been published in various magazines and anthologies. Her published work includes seven books for children, including *A Sky Black with Crows*. She wrote *A Long Way from Home* after listening to stories from people who were involved with the diverted 9/11 passengers.